Viola
in
Waiting

Sandra Rubini-Rochon

For Louie and Mac

One

Viola Waits

Bay Port, Michigan

10 May 1898

Viola waits.

Dusk descends upon another sultry Huron eve and still she waits, as rendered by virtue of ceremony. Enduring the motions of yet another vernal equinox, tilling the compost of unpretentious gardens bearing the whole of her sustenance.

Viola delves knowing fingers into the moist, ebony soil of her family homestead which has bourne witness to the love and loss of three generations of the Giordano Clan. No gloves interfere with this pure and raw joining, as she favours manipulating such bounty with bare hands. The sweet fruits of labour beget man's unification with earth.

Viola lovingly tucks the last of the indoor starts into the soil, a practice taught by Mother to ensure seedlings remain strong enough to survive Michigan's unpredictable climate. Although spring has descended in a mild fashion this season, it only takes one cold snap to ruin months of work and crop, and sowing bare seed early on by the bay has proven a risky affair. It is a habit of good measure, and a tradition of which there is no sense to break.

Viola firmly secures a stake next to each start and sets back on her haunches to make certain they've been placed in a straight and handsome line. Oak branches from the thick of the glen were gathered last fall and whittled over long winter days with Father's old bowie knife. Many afternoons were spent in his rocker on the front porch, quietly shaping and reshaping the lovely limbs, daydreaming of the sweet corn, tomatoes, okra, and fuzzy cucumber tentacles that would cling to them for support barely six months from that very moment. She remembers taking pause to stare at the blinding blanket of snow protecting the dormant earth, with nothing but sparrows and the methodical drip! drip! drip! of melting icicles on the eaves to keep her company, to witness many of the musings she spoke aloud.

Viola stands to brush her knees and make a final survey of her work for the day. This is the second of three plantings, the first having concluded last month by advice of The Almanac. Its teachings have given Viola much confidence in her horticulture abilities over the years, blessing her with the wisdom to respect all aspects of nature during planting season. How important it is to be patient for the correct signs; to be cognizant of the waxing and waning lunar cycles – the danger in their mixed blessings when combined with an individual's poor planning. Last month's plantings were conducted under the cool and dry earth sign of Taurus, favoring of perennials and root crop - sweet potatoes, yams, sugar beets and carrots.

This time around – on the cusp of hot and arid Gemini -

lovely spearmint for evening tea; soybeans, peppers, peas, asparagus, which hopefully will not fall victim to the dreaded rot wilt as in years past; and the sweet corn, cucumbers, okra, and tomatoes, of course. Plus, squash of several varieties, zucchini being her favorite.

Next month will come the plantings under the most fertile sign of the Zodiac, the cool and moist water sign of Cancer, most gracious to crops of the green leafy variety - Swiss chard, chicory, arugula, spinach, and collard, mustard, and dandelion greens. Viola's plantings the end of May and into June have always bourne the most luscious crops of all, and the fire sign of Leo the most barren. The Almanac offers foreboding of July and August as the poorest months of the year for planting or harvest, as seed will shrivel and perish.

Viola returns the implements to their pegs in the faded red barn, a weathered and stoic monarch which has long since fallen into charming disrepair along with the back pastures and eighty wooded acres ending their graceful sway on the shores of The Great Huron. Pastures once accommodating hundreds of cattle are now home to only six or seven at any given time.

And today, as each day at the end of her toil, Viola strolls the well-worn, narrow path through bursting fields of gold, down past overgrown patches of briar and sumac to the edge of the oak glen and beyond. She makes her way ceremoniously through the shaded wood, whose rocky soils surrender to honey-textured sand and pebble, and fragments of shell and driftwood and bone. And it is here, every day, where Viola waits.

The lake is tepid and calm this May eve. Already the suns of the past month have set a glowing ochre fury on the horizon, that fine line separating water and sky increasingly murky and diluted each day in the growing warmth. Already the chickpeas and potatoes have sprouted, and Viola hopes The Good Mother is kind this year, conceding her rime until the coming fall.

Viola breathes deeply. The earthy humus of decaying leaves. Fresh water, abundant of fish and crustacean. Pure air and sky and low-lying cloud awhirl on the gentle breeze fill her lungs.

She lifts linen skirts above her ankles to make herself comfortable on the bare sand and straightens her spine, stretching arms to the violet sky to relish the ache of her labours, the tingle of blood rushing from fingertips to torso. Fine lines and creases in aging hands are curiously examined, soil and wisdom baked deep beneath the nails. Once these hands were tender and smooth, lacking spidery wisps and callused edges. *But that was long ago, in what seems another lifetime.*

When Robert died, much of Viola's heart perished with him - that luscious element of youth so heartbreakingly pure and fleeting - that intangible innocence and lust for life which fuels passion and reckless abandon. And sometimes, when the day sets in that similar manner - when the sun simmers amidst a throbbing haze of heat and stale stagnation - that's when Viola catches her breath. That's when the tang of earth, water, and sky - mingled with the memory of burning wood, hot ash and flesh - quickens the very fibre of her marrow so swiftly she nearly gags.

Viola surveys the boundless stretch of deserted beach both east and west. Sandpipers, gulls, and scurrying crayfish are her family now, treating her with casual disregard though ever-aware of her presence. She unlaces her square-toed half boots and sweaty woolen socks, discarding them as an

afterthought, and buries thankful toes into the warm sand.
She dislodges a tiny mollusk shell which she tucks in her
apron pocket. A dozen of the same (though as snowflakes,
no two quite identical) dangle from twine on the porch eve.

Perhaps she'll make another.
And then again,
perhaps not.

The sun delves into a deeper hue of early-summer ire,
transforming clear sky and tufts of cumulous cover into a
brilliant pallet of fuchsia and sienna, and deeper still.
Glimmers of star shine join the visual chorus in the promise
of full dusk, the peace of all-encompassing darkness.

Amidst a show of flickering fireflies, Viola decides to sit a
while longer.

Tonight, Viola waits.

V

We shall meet, but we shall miss him
There will be one vacant chair...

Viola's eyes flutter open. Huron is reflecting the day's
last waning light as it slides unceremoniously into obscurity,
and she estimates having been asleep for an hour or so. She
rubs her eyes and settles upon the swaying bend of coastline
leading toward town, and the luminous Bay Port Hotel.

We shall linger to caress him
While we breathe our evening prayer...

Languid flutters of lyric, akin to dawdling dust motes, hover in the shadows, their testament of yearning so vague she doubts their origin. And reminiscent of the subtle scent of a woman in passing, a whisper yet remains, leaving one to ponder their existence at all.

When a year ago we gathered
Joy was in his mild blue eye...

But a golden chord is severed
And our hopes in ruin lie ...

"*They go,*" she whispers.

Two

Market Day

11 May 1898

Fat Henry's song in the coop rouses Viola promptly at 4:50 AM, as it has for almost two years now. A proud and ruffled Araucana cock is he, strutting feathered perfection about the barnyard each morning with a loyal, though scatter-brained harem in tow.

Viola rubs sleep from her eyes with balled fists like a child as she ambles toward the casement, pushing aside a lace sash to peer at the full moon shedding its transcendental glow upon wheat fields in the paling night. Two deer, mother and fawn, take their breakfast of sweet grass on the edge of the glen. Sensing movement, the doe momentarily raises her head to study Viola before resuming eager nibbles.

Fat Henry and his flock rustle inside the coop, awaiting daybreak before venturing outside so as not to fall prey to the final roamings of coyotes slinking into dens for the day.

Viola shuffles to the armoire and removes a white cotton night robe from its oak hanger, releasing the musky redolence of lavender as she pulls the garment over her head.

Lavender sachets, stuffed and stitched by hand from swatches of surplus fabric, are tucked into drawers and wardrobes, just as Mother had done, and Nonna before her.

Viola moves to her bureau and gazes into the mirror, once again shocked by her image.

Bontà! When did this happen? Who is this forty-year-old woman staring back at me with a striking resemblance to Mother?

Within she remains that giddy sixteen-year-old accepting Robert Thompson's bent-kneed proposal on starlit Wild Foul Bay - but externally, Mother Nature continues her wanton assault on vain sensibilities.

Not that she is unattractive - *al contrario!* Farm labours keep her hard and trim, staying the folds of middle-age in abeyance. Breasts round and firm, not having succumbed to the indignity of gravity. And though lines about her mouth and eyes deepen just slightly each year, Viola's skin remains resilient. A spatter of freckles dance about her nose and cheeks, deceiving one into the opinion she is not a day past thirty years. And though long curly black hair is fading, it retains its thick and vital elasticity, the tone and texture of fine oriental silk.

"Madra Naura, thy will be done."

Viola sighs as she walks downstairs to the kitchen to kindle a modest fire in the well-worn hearth of sooty river rock. A cast iron kettle of water and coffee grounds simmers on a hook above the flames as she slips into Father's tanned-hide Wellingtons, which are a might roomy, but not exceedingly so. Her feet were always much larger than those of the other girls in town, and they certainly let her know it! At five-foot, eight-inches tall, she towered above most of them. How cruel children can be, honing in on the differences and perceived weaknesses in others, and here she is thirty-three years later, still feeling a twinge of that ridicule.

Viola retrieves a near-empty bag of rolled oats purchased at Market last month and simmers them in a cast iron pot that belonged to her great-grandmother. Three strips of cured bacon are pulled from the rack in the pantry and sizzle furiously as she drops them gingerly into the hot skillet.

The kettle begins to sputter, and Viola removes the steaming vessel from the hearth to strain a cup of coffee through tightly knit cheesecloth, the same type of cloth used to wrap balls of dough before molding them into crust for venison and blackberry pies. Some of the grounds escape the cloth but are lost in the hearty bitterness. She is nearly drained of beans - and flour and sugar and most other household staples.

First day of the month. Market Day for Viola Thompson.

Viola pulls the kettle from the hearth and pours hot water into the kitchen wash basin, where she rinses each pot and utensil. One-by-one, she places them into the water; one-by-one she methodically wipes the inside of each pan. Slow, circular motions, enjoying the steady comfort of the familiar; the quiet; the instant gratification of another clean pot, another shining silver fork. She fans her fingers into the cooling water and observes them curiously. Slow and steady she wipes the next plate before adding fresh warm kettle water.

Something catches Viola's eye, and she lifts her head to look through the kitchen window directly in front of her. A magnificent Rufous hummingbird floating in mid-air, just on the other side of the pane, observing her with the same curiosity. She marvels at the flurry of white and amber feathers, fragile and slick like smooth, wet silk. Miniscule black pinpricks for eyes, stoic and unwavering.

Viola smiles and the little bird departs with a whirling buzz.

"Like a giant bee," she says aloud.

Viola fills her mug with coffee and carries it to the porch as the sun ascends the crest of the bluff in a glorious stratum of crimson laurel. The doe and child still linger in the field, though having edged closer to the comfort of the wood, and Fat Henry and his harem waddle one-by-one from the coop, ruffling and clucking their greetings to Viola, and dawn.

Viola carries a pine bucket of feed to the hungry brood, scattering it about the compact dirt in front of the coop and gently clucking back to them under her breath. As they readily take to pecking the stock, she collects their eggs from the roost. She will sell or trade them at Market in town today.

Market Day was always an event in the Giordano household. Viola would listen to her parents stir in their room down the hall, the bedroom she now calls her own. Shortly after the rooster's first crow, as she lay in pre-dawn slumber with eyes still closed, Mother's soft step would pass by the door … one … two … three … four … and familiar rustlings would resume in the kitchen directly below her bedroom. Searching through the pantry for coffee grounds and wheat flour … removing the cast iron skillet and kettle from their hooks above the hearth … the screen door opening and banging softly as il gatto was let outside for his morning hunt. The comforting sounds and smells of home, of love and warmth. Of childhood.

After breakfast Father would rise from the table and stretch, patting his stomach with satisfaction. And every morning without fail he would turn to his lovely wife and smile, thanking her for the bountiful breakfast, brushing a gentle kiss against her left cheek before winking at his two children and disappearing out the back door to feed the goats and horses. Viola and little Anthonie would help Mother clear the table and tidy the kitchen before hurrying upstairs with that knot of anticipation in their bellies, for Market Day in the Giordano household was quite an event.

Once upstairs, Mother would help her children select their Sunday best. Viola always chose the same outfit to wear on Market Day, and closing her eyes now could see it stitch for stitch as if she were still eight years old. The blue and white cotton smock Mother finished last spring. The frilly white blouse and lacey knickers which tickled her ankles so! Calf-high leather lace-ups. A fancy straw hat with a big yellow bow. "Very beautiful!" ladies at Market would smile. Anthonie received most of that attention now - as most four-year-olds will - filling Viola with a tinge of envy, but mostly just pride and adoration.

Viola opens her eyes and scans the armoire for the outfit she now wears as an adult. A pale rose skirt of linen, burgundy bodice, and cotton cream blouse with faux pearl buttons and a modest collar of sculpted lace. She pulls each garment from its hanger and eyes them thoughtfully before placing them on the bed and retrieving her floppy straw hat, minus the yellow bow.

After dressing, Viola stands at her kitchen chopping block and reads through her list for a second time. One last scan of cupboards and pantry and a few last-minute scribbles before going out to the barn.

"Here you go sweetie." Viola offers Carl a sliver of dried apple from fall harvest which she keeps stashed in her apron pockets. "Come're, love."

The burro ambles meekly forward, anticipation evident in the fervent swish! swish! of his tufted tail. She places the fruit in her flat palm and Carl's eager lips nibble at the delectable treat, his plump tongue wet and sloppy across her fingers and wrist. She scratches between the lengthy elegance of coarse ears, and he offers his appreciation as a grunt and tender nudge to her hip.

"Let's put this on you, then."

Viola slings the crocheted hemp pannier over Carl's back to rest on either side of his bulging mid-frame paunch before making several trips to the house to gather all her trading goods.

✓ *Six dozen eggs from the girls, wrapped in burlap and tied with dainty twine bows.*

✓ *Two dozen lavender wands, woven from dried stalks of lavender and sweet grass.*

✓ *Seven elephant bulb garlic braids from last fall's harvest.*

✓ *Two dozen muslin bath pouches – dried rosemary, lavender, mint, chamomile, lemon verbena and sweet woodruff, mixed with powdered milk and oatmeal.*

✓ *Twelve mason jars of vinegar, her own homemade concoction of oregano, thyme, dill, and garlic – with a splash of bell pepper for pizzazz!*

✓ *Three dozen pinecone fire starters, laced with lavender and rosemary and soaked in melted paraffin scraps.*

✓ *Three dozen tallow-based bathing bars, scented with a divine concoction of clove, geranium, sandalwood, oak moss, rose and bergamot.*

✓ *And three of her latest oil paintings, lovely pastoral landscapes created on lazy spring mornings on the front porch.*

When Viola has securely stowed away her goods in Carl's pannier pockets, she slings Father's rustic leather haversack over her left shoulder. At Market she will exchange goods with vendors of choice, swelling each pouch with sufficient staples to carry her through another month.

As Carl chaws the apple, Viola fastens a relaxed harness and lead over his muzzle and guides him down the half-mile trail toward the dirt thoroughfare to town.

Viola cautiously hugs the shoulder to defer ample right-of way to the occasional wagon or passing carriage. The hawser lead is held loosely in one hand as she and Carl walk side-by-side, more so resembling amiable comrades than Mistress and Beast.

She detects the approach of a wagon around the bend, and

before she can turn to consider its occupants or taste the dry and bitter trace of road dust on her lips, she recognizes the familiar squeal and scrape of the right rear wheel. The Iverson Clan. Joshua and wife, Monica. Jeb and Diana, their two teenage children.

Though the wagon has served the family well over the years, it has certainly seen better days, and Viola can't help but muse that the poor old hag is on its last leg. The wheels wobble and lurch, as do the wagon's inhabitants as they rest upon hard plank seats fitted loosely inside. Only a whisper of washed-out red remains in the cracks and crevices of splintered grey. And side rails, loosely fitted with frayed hemp, appear much too fragile to contain their cargo - especially the type of load Joshua always seems to haul, as though compensating for other shortcomings.

Joshua is Viola's senior by only one year. Their fathers worked together "Back in the Days of Soo," as Father called it, a time in the 1850's when the two men were members of the crew that constructed the Soo Locks in Marquette. After a few nips of Old Overholt around the campfire, Father and Mr. Iverson often told tales of this time in their lives quite fondly. Of the exhausting labour, comradery and isolation, and the dread of losing several dear friends to the horrific cholera epidemic that swept through the camps with merciless ferocity, wiping out one fourth of the workforce in less than two weeks.

The Giordano and Iverson clans were quite friendly for many years, taking Sunday suppers or picnics together at least once every month or two. "Until," as Father would scowl many times in subsequent years, "the day of Mr. Iverson's incomprehensible duplicity - an unforgivable lapse of judgment and irrefutable flaw of character." Family suppers and picnics ceased abruptly. Viola never understood what transpired until many years later when she ran into Old Man Iverson in town, just a couple years ago, before his passing. They exchanged a smile and nod between them, and though no specifics were spoken, she caught a whisper of "knowing" from Mr. Iverson - that wide breadth of subtle urgency occasionally emanating from the auras of those close to death. Those on the path to owning their regrets and eager for opportunities to make amends. Antonello Giordano's blood ran through her veins - the blood of a man Mr. Iverson once loved - which made her a direct vessel to atonement. "I am so sorry, dear girl," he whispered to Viola. "I live remorseful having allowed my lowly humanness to get the better of me. I hope you can forgive me."

All she could do was smile and shake her head at the thought of this eighty-seven-year-old man trying to bed her own mother, his best friend's wife. *Oh my...*

And it has been told (by those who tell such things), that the apple of Mrs. Iverson's eye had not fallen far from the tree himself, as one of Joshua's escapades had town all a titter for months. He had apparently gotten quite pickled one night and found himself racing said wagon down the thoroughfare at precarious speeds, until it crashed ass-over-teakettle and inflicted enough harm to one of the nags that the poor beast had to be put down on the spot. It was said that Monica was so enraged by the incident she banished Joshua to the barn with the goats and sheep for near a month, until he vowed to give up drink and beg the Lord's forgiveness by attending church with her and the children every Sunday. Whenever Viola reflected upon Monica prior to The Incident, she beheld a hard, unattractive woman - homely some might say. But after that night, Viola saw

Monica Iverson in a whole new light. She held her head high, an inner beauty bourne of pride and strength. Monica Iverson was not about to take such business from the likes of Joshua Iverson - or anyone else for that matter. And she insisted he not fix the wheel damaged in The Incident, to let it remain a constant reminder of past sordid ways, and the Higher Path chosen.

As they pass, Joshua touches the brim of his felt fedora and nods, and his smile is broad and genuine.

Viola recalls the two of them racing up and down the beach as children. *"Tag! You're IT!"* he'd giggle, in that ratchety pre-pubescent squeal of twelve-year-old-boydom. They'd while away the days without a care in the world, chasing, tagging, rolling along the dunes until sundown. Viola nods in return, and wonders if he's musing about the beach as well, about those endless summer afternoons.

Monica bids a cordial nod, and the children consider her curiously from the rear of the wagon, sitting atop fifty-pound sacks of Washburn Crosby Gold Medal Wheat Flour and munching *Toddy Arnold's Kettle Corn - Made While-U-Wait!* After passing a respectful distance, the familial pageant quickens its pace, fading amidst a plume of dust and clopping hooves.

Viola had always been proud of her parents' wagon. Nothing fancy, but very trim and clean, as Father and Mother took impeccable care of what little they had. That lovely little wagon had been passed down to her and Robert after they wed and now sat in dusty ruin, rotting away in one of the barn stalls. It had last been driven five years ago, before she sold Father's stallions to buy food and staples to see her through the first winter after Father's death and to purchase supplies to fix the dilapidated fencing and install barbed wire to contain what few cattle remained.

Viola contemplates the fingers of her left hand, which still bear the scars from that installation; the gashes and blisters that festered and took months to heal. Over the years she pondered selling the wagon, as it would fetch a handsome price, but she had never been able to do so.

Viola turns her attentions to the roadside terrain which completely transforms each time she makes the trek into town. Last July when the wild roses were in bloom, she had stuffed her pockets full of their sweet petals, which she uses to make rosewater to scent herself after bathing, or infusions to cure whatever happened to be ailing her at the time. When combined with chamomile and lavender, a sure-fire cure for insomnia; or when ingested straight and pure, an essential restoration and stimulation of vital energy. This month, barberry and hazel thickets sprout about fields' edge. Sweet wild carrot and fennel extend in unbridled profusion, the latter lending a peppery splash of licorice flavouring to her stews.

Viola looks up and is surprised that she has already come upon the Ice Age monolith "Big Rock," which signifies they are less than a quarter mile from town. She makes mental note to pause on the way back for clippings.

As the stretch of road widens just a few steps beyond Big Rock, the distant buzz of civilization intensifies. The low hum of activity begins to reverberate in her chest, and she breaks into a cool sweat. She pauses to kick at a deep wagon rut entrenched in the earth and bends over to pick up a small stone. Carl looks up inquisitively and brushes against her hand with his cool nose. *He feels it.* The stone slips from Viola's trembling grasp as she takes the burro's muzzle in both hands. His ears twitch reflexively at her touch.

The Ambush, as Viola refers to it, though descending with much less frequency than in years past, continues to rear its ugliness when least expected or convenient. Waiting in line at the bank or commenting to an acquaintance at Market concerning the inflated cost of melon, it arrives, a presence so intrinsically sublime. A hungry tick latching to gorge at the base of the spine, embedding itself as a raw thought, a subtle glance or gesture. A mere tickle brushed away, a tittering annoyance. The expedient progression of blood surging to temples … vertigo … hyperventilation … a numbing fog and unmitigated weariness … the tang of metallic deposited upon the tongue.

One deep breath ... close your eyes ... exhale, slowly...

The Ambush slowly creeps its way from her belly like a plump, juicy leech, sucking its way through her chest cavity and esophagus to lodge in her throat,

(deep jagged breath ... exhale, slowly)

feeding on slick tissue,

(deep breath ... exhale, slowly ...)

and it explodes - a victim of its own greedy, unquenchable thirst.

Viola knows if she opens her eyes during this exhalation process, she is certain to see tiny spatters of blood drifting through her lips and floating on the breeze until they disperse like miniscule motes through a sunbeam.

No longer Viola Thompson, merely an androgynous vessel.

Host.
Matriarch.
Pariah.

And a woman's soul screams through its attempts to abscond the chasm of bleak malevolence, until finally it erupts through her pores a billion tiny particles of frenzied chaos into The Light ...

Viola opens her eyes.

Once The Ambush has passed, she is purged – or exorcized, to some extent – and is able to regain composure. Even so, its presence will linger, sometimes for days, like the aura of a bad headache. For you see, though one may remove the tick, many times the head remains. Burrowing. Mechanically feasting without apparent rhyme or purpose.
"Let's go sweetie," she whispers to Carl, and they resume their journey, side-by-side, into town.

V

Viola guides Carl along the winding path, wide enough now for carriages to pass through on either side. Remnants of winter's muddy ruts still remain. They walk across the old Unionville Trestle built above Wallace Slough. Wood planks sound loud as carriages pass over them, bouncing the boards beneath their feet. A stagecoach rolls by on its way to the Bay Port Hotel. There used to be dozens traveling the roads of Bay Port, but they are a rare sight now that the train depot has arrived.

Farms encompass the land, a colorful patchwork of fields in shades of green, yellow and brown, cordoned off by barbed wire, with brush and wildflowers growing at their edges. Each field is different. Some are bare dirt, others wheat or corn, using oxen and scythe to work the earth. Some of the larger farms are now using machines called threshers to cut the harvest - a dreadful beast snorting black smoke into the pure air.

Barns of all shapes and sizes dot the land here. Some made of splintered knotty pine with swallows swirling gracefully around high-pitched roofs. Others with weathered cobblestone foundations and maple structures. The Cooper farm to the left has always been one of Viola's favorites, looking as though it had just come out of a fairytale. Tall poplars protect the property on the wind side. Chickens mill about and atop bales of hay, and an old grey barn cat watches them, rather disinterested, from the wrap around porch. A marshy creek runs between the house and barn with a small bridge that Grandpa Cooper had built when she was a child. Grasses and cattails are prolific around its edge.

Another farm down the way a bit – the Steadman Farm – is in charming stages of disrepair. Barns with thatched roofs, fraying at the edges, with wobbly hand-blown glass windows, rusted implements and old mine equipment from the limestone quarry. Two silos made of stone surrounded by fallen leaves from old black cherry and apple trees. Viola remembers one time years ago, when the land was still a working farm, that one of the hands became trapped in a silo. He fell in and was enveloped and smothered by grain.

Viola and Carl continue toward town, cresting a slight gradient in the road which affords a rolling view of rooftops

on approach. Buildings become more densely clustered
here. Cottages of cobbled river stone, brick and pine boards
in shades of grey, beige, brown and white, with jagged
mortar crooks and crannies. Picket fences with patches of
wildflowers, acylium and crabgrass sprouting from cracks of
concrete and brick entry retainer walls. Elm trees, oak and
maple line the streets.

The closer one gets to town, the fancier the houses
become. Victorian homes with mansard towers and portable
dormers, iron roof cresting and tall first floor windows.
Stately wrought iron gates and brick pathways leading to
front doors surrounded by large verandas and willow-treed
gardens. All lined up next to one another like good little
soldiers, fortresses of safety for their inhabitants.

Viola enters town, which is always bustling on Market
Day. Mid-morning services at the Methodist Church have
just let out, and people spill through the huge entry doors
into the streets, thanking the pastor and bidding one another
a good day. The courthouse is directly across the street,
three levels high with a clock tower and flag posts, a stately,
official-looking building built in the 1840's Gothic style.
Next to that the Bayview Township hall has voting booths,
town meetings, dances, weddings and wakes. Most of the
buildings have pitched roofs with gables and are made of
brick or asphalt in muted colors of white, brown, blue, grey.
Fancy light posts line the streets, which are lit by hand in the
evenings – though the first electric lines are making this
practice obsolete. They run parallel down the road through
town, bringing electricity to the small commercial district.
The poles were made from old growth remaining after The
Big Fire, and glass insulators reflect afternoon sunlight.
Some of the wealthy residents are tying into it as well.

On the other side of town, on First Street across from the canal, are the Gillingham Fish Company, built in 1886, and the Bay Port Fish Company built in 1895. These buildings encompass a little ecosystem of their own, a fishing port and village, a commercial operation of perch, walleye, herring, whitefish and carp shipped to Detroit, Chicago and New York. There are little shanty buildings with shingled roofs, chimney stacks and flues banging in the wind. A dock with a long wharf and weathered dories tied along its length. Barrels, pilings, buoys and buckets. Wooden crates and handmade fish nets, hung to dry. Men bustling everywhere donning caps, suspenders and boots.

Viola pauses to watch the men untangling fish nets on the dock. She loves the way they throw themselves into their work. One of the men notices her. He is short and portly, a cigar cocked into the crook of his mouth. He raises his hand to lift his cap in her direction and smiles. She smiles back.

"Okay, Carl," she says. "Time to join the masses."

The Bay Port Town Market on Lakeside Drive lasts from sunup to sundown. It is a necessity for everyday life essentials, and most everyone within a ten-mile radius attends at some point or another during the day. Although town merchants carried many of the goods one needed, the fresh meats and produce could only be obtained this one day of the month. Wares and tinctures of the freshest variety. Density bustling unparalleled anywhere else in the otherwise laziness of quietude the other twenty-nine days per month.

Viola stops at the edge of The Market. She closes her

eyes and then opens them again to find herself staring at a second-floor window of the Bay Port State Bank building. The four square panes are separated by milled slats of pine, their rounded edges not so much seen at this distance, rather known. They are a tad wavy, dimensional, and Viola imagines when the late day sun shines upon them, they reflect her light as prisms of the spectrum. The white paint is beginning to peel.

Viola squints and blurs her vision, concentrating her focus on the center of the wooden pane cross. Though hazy, she is grounded and centered, hyper-aware of her surroundings and indifferent to how she must appear to others around her – a frozen, crazy fool.

The morning sun is warm upon her shoulders and the top of her bodice, reminding her of the contrast posed by the cool ilk of bourbon as it quietly spreads its fingers through one's chest. Liquid Sunshine, they say. *Sole Liquido.*

Carl shifts his weight from left to right, enjoying the warmth as well – or irritated by it. She can't tell.

The low-grade buzz Viola had felt in her chest has erupted into a chasm of collective humanity, stimulating the senses. She takes it all in. Voices bartering, inquiring; the banter of baritones and falsettos - some light, others more serious. Contradictions at play, from loud and obnoxious to gentle and accommodating. Aggressive conjecture, to snippets full of pleases and thank yous; how muches and how manys. Laughter everywhere. People happy to be out of the house, walking in the sunshine and socializing. Gossip, invitations to dinner, recounting recent physical woes and exchanging recipes. A wave of warmth from grilled food. The rustle of women's bustles. A man's cane hitting the ground in rhythmic intervals. Chickens and yapping dogs. Banjo and bluegrass lilt uptown from the end of the block, Tommy Lee's wobbly twang weaving a tale of "lost love passing through Virginia way." The hurried steps of children running alongside their parents, whoopin' and hollerin' to '*Wait up! Can I try? I'm gonna tell Momma!*' Giggling in front of penny candy barrels, *Ten Strips of Licorice for a Cent!* And through all the clutter, Viola can hear, most of all, Robin song. Singing their hearts out in the treetops. Do they speak to one another through their joyous melody? What can their messages be? I love you, dear? Meet me at Mud Lake for a dousing? Found a good worm patch in the Johnson's yard? Or perhaps they are merely giving thanks for the glorious day and the sunshine. Viola is curious to know if she is the only one, right here, right now, to notice them, to behold the only thing that truly matters.

"Therefore, thus says the Lord!"

A disheveled man bumps into Viola, shocking her back from her reflections. His hair and beard are overgrown, and his general appearance dirty, chaotic. He wears a goatee, holding himself with brimstone and angst, seeming to regard the rest of the world with slight contempt.

"Behold! I am bringing disaster upon them that they cannot escape! Though they cry to me, I will not listen to them!"

He carries a crooked staff made of oak and waves it about while flailing his arms and moving into the crowd churning around lines of bright tents and booths clogging the main street.

"Then we who are left will be caught up together in the clouds to meet the Lord in the air! Therefore, stay awake, for you do not know on what day your Lord is coming!"

Viola guides Carl in the opposite direction toward Millard

Pantome's display of stationery, ink wells and quills. A luxury, for certain, but one she tends to indulge in at least once every couple of years. The quills are fashioned from exotic ostrich feathers that Millard's brother sends from Australia. Whenever Viola creates ink drawings, they are somehow so much better with a quill and ink, rather than blocky charcoal sticks. An artist is all about internal perception – which can be a blessing or a curse. Millard loves her vinegars, so she should be able to get a good trade with him.

Across from Millard's setup is Tammy Finney and her husband, Michael. Tammy is one of only a few women in town who always smiles and waves when their paths cross. She is a true, nonjudgmental Christian woman, very heavily involved in the Methodist Church. She's not at the booth right now, but Michael is showing a couple customers one of the exquisite steel knives he milled in his forge, with deer antler handles. His display is quite handsome, full of knives, leather harnesses, steel jewelry and smoked fish. Tammy has an equally engaging display of her work co-mingled with Michael's. Wool from her Wensleydales spun into cantaloupe-sized balls, dyed lovely shades of pink, crème, light blue, and violet. Spice jars, trinkets made from Petosky stones and glass, heirloom brooches and tallow candles. And this is where she first sees him.

His dress is different, obviously not from around this area. He wears a long leather duster which is worn and frayed around the edges. It is washed out and a bit wrinkled in places, having seen a lot of travel over the years, as have his dusty boots and faded dungarees. He wears a slouch hat, and a worn haversack is slung over one shoulder with a small blanket rolled up and secured to the bottom of it by wide leather straps. The case he carries in his left hand is beat up. *Looks like it's been through a lot,* she contemplates, *as does he.*

The stranger is very tall – at least six-foot-two - with a firm and muscular frame, offering those of discerning taste – of either sex - little choice but to take notice. His gait is fluid and natural, full of lithe confidence. And what appears to be a faint whisper of cool mystery trails behind him, akin to the lazy swirl of wafting cigar smoke. Of course this mystery, Viola muses, is most likely the result of nothing more than his status as a stranger in town. Any out-of-place face in these parts draws attention.

Two courtly young women in their Sunday best pass by the stranger as he stops to inspect a rack of hanging jerky. They pause behind him and glance over his backside, immediately turning to one another with goo-goo eyes and covering hushed giggles as they skitter away.

Viola rolls her eyes.

Her attention is drawn to a row of honey melons stacked in a pyramid of tidy spheres. They're early this year. She cradles one with both hands and gently knocks on it. When she looks up again, the stranger has turned, and is staring at her.

Viola's chest tightens, and a pause or two lapse before she is conscious of holding her breath. When their eyes lock, she is compelled to look away, but cannot. And though the brim of his hat lightly shades his features from full view, she is acutely aware of gentle laugh lines framing what appear to be kind and playful eyes; a coarse salt and pepper moustache above full pink lips; and the chiseled stubble of at least a fortnight or two. *My Lord, he's beautiful.* He nods in greeting, and she drops her eyes, turning away.

"How much for the melon?" she asks the merchant.

Viola purchases two. As she stuffs them into Carl's pannier, she looks back toward the jerky display, and the stranger is gone.

Three

Ghosts

Viola rests on the porch at twilight's wane after a supper of venison stew, methodically keeping time in the same Mission rocker where Mother soothed her as a child. She absent-mindedly stares into daylight's languid decline, attempting her damndest to quell a rising disturbance.

Henry rounds up the gals and steers them toward the roost. They waddle up the tapered wooden plank a single-file brood of clucking feathers and attitude, where they will vanish until dawn.

Viola rises and clasps her hands at the small of her back as she begins to pace the porch.

Since the reappearance of The Ambush earlier that day, a constant unnerving murmur of undistinguishable dialogue lay waste to her calm. Her mind jumps fro and hence amidst a rush of flashing images that are irrational in content, happenstance in chronology. She grasps for one to hone in on in an effort to stop the spinning and lands upon a memory five years ago when her younger brother Anthonie visited for a spell, six months or so after Father's death.

Anthonie had bid farewell to his family in Seattle and

traveled alone to Michigan by steam engine and stagecoach. Viola was shocked by the grey at his temples and deep laugh lines around his eyes, and she sensed the same subtle surprise reflected in him as well. It had been the first time they'd seen one another in nearly eighteen years.

A connoisseur of hard and fancy spirits from the tender age of nine, Anthonie did not disappoint on this unexpected visit to the homestead. He readily hopped off the carriage with a boisterous embrace and proceeded to rummage through a leather travel bag damn near big as the state of Texas, producing an amber fifth of Snowflake Whiskey in either hand and beaming a grin as long and wide as the Mason Dixon Line. The driver hopped down from the coach and helped him retrieve a huge wooden crate stamped Hall, Luhrs & CoS in bold black letters. "A gift from Out West!" The two of them greeted many dawns during his month-long stay, fueled by drink and the reminiscence of times past.

Anthonie lived the life of wonder and adventure Viola had always fancied. At seventeen he was lured by the sirens of The West and ventured to the great northern miner's town of Windham Bay in the lustful pursuit of wealth. It was in this forlorn little miner's camp southeast of Juneau where he made his fortune and met six-foot-two Matilda, camp cook and wife of fifteen years. 'All Woman!' he'd told Viola with a twinkle in his eye. His descriptions conjured images of a towering blonde Viking wench, sheer muscle and sass.

Anthonie decided to make the journey to Bay Port after receiving Viola's written account of Father's death. His headstrong mission was to help her sell the homestead and move back to Seattle with him and Matilda and their four children.

"What is left here for you Viola, other than sad

memories?"

And though immensely persuasive, Anthonie was no match for Viola's will. When he left, alone and disappointed, she knew it would probably be the last time she would ever see her brother.

One bottle of Anthonie's Snowflake rests upon the top shelf in the pantry behind the canning supplies. Viola had forgotten about it, for the most part, passing over it on occasion when rummaging for mason jars and lids.

The screen door slams behind her as she enters the kitchen and scratches a wooden matchstick against the limestone countertop next to the washbasin. She removes the hurricane flute from one of her oil lanterns and gently touches match to wick to soften evening shadows before dragging a chair into the pantry.

The amber bottle is cool and covered with a fine film of age. Viola carries it to the butcher block in the center of the kitchen and reaches for an empty jelly jar before popping the cork. She fills the jar to the rim and raises it to her lips, closing her eyes as liquid comfort glides down her throat, gradually dispersing its soothing ilk through her chest and stomach like thick, warm tentacles of molasses. Her mind begins to wander again, and she is taken aback by an overwhelming reflection of Robert.

Waking in the wan morning light in a bed much too vast, where once the warmth of his body was a reassurance taken for granted. The creak of springs as he slid his legs over the side of the mattress; the shuffle of tired feet into the kitchen and slam! of the screen door as he stumbled toward the privy, rubbing sleep from his eyes. Sometimes Viola would roll into the spot he'd vacated to await his return. She could still feel his warmth and the smell of him, of oat grass and sweet wood smoke. Of Robert.

Where once lived the vital breadth of her husband, only cool and sterile linens remain. Though it is not the same bed they had shared, Viola hasn't occupied Robert's side since his passing, as if an unspeakable barrier lies down the center of the mattress, and some sacred sense of – *respect?* – *despair? – fear?* – prevents her from doing so, even in slumber.

Viola carries the bottle outside and squats upon the stoop. Watching. Waiting. *But waiting for what?* For Robert to stroll up the walk in those chalky old catchalls, baggy and dusted with limestone from Wallace Quarry?

He had a carefree amble, Robert did, a way about him that made one inclined to tweak his cheeks and invite him to supper. It was mostly his smile, Viola remembers, or maybe that wild burst of chocolate curl. Tall as a beanpole; bright, gentle, smiling. Yes, always smiling.

And the soot was everywhere! But Viola didn't mind. She didn't mind drawing a bath in the barn for him every night, positioning the basin in that brilliant orange triangle of evening glow. Viola would wash his back with a scrubber and lavender lye soap. She'd hum and rub him real gentle, and he would rest there in the basin, tired and hunched, hugging his knees to his chest and telling her how much he'd missed her all day, how much he loved her. Sometimes Viola would wake the next morning to find a little smudge of limestone powder across the bridge of her nose, or calf – or on her fanny even! And she'd always giggle.

Ashes to ashes.

Viola refills the empty jar and carries it with her to the barn. Umber evening light floods through the open back door. She strolls the stalls, checking on the cows and Carl. The burrow swishes his tail with gratitude as she slips him a cup of grain before crossing the blazing threshold en route to the branded beach trail, rendered threadbare by countless tramplings over the decades. Mother, Father, Anthonie, Robert, Nonna Isabelle, Nonno Elio, many aunts, uncles and countless cousins and family friends. Viola has walked the path so many times she could do so blindfolded in the dead of a moonless night.

This time, at the trail's 'Y,' she turns right, taking the path less traveled toward the bluff, a route nowhere near defined as the other.

This had been Mother's Sacred Place, the end of the earth where sky meets timeless expanse of dune, water, and meadow, where gulls float eye level on the crest of a mild jet stream.

Here, Mother and Father lay side-by-side, their headstones identical. Carved of bland limestone, simple and stoic; gritty and sterile. Only the names and dates distinguish them from one another.

Viola had tried her best to accommodate Father, to fill the void in his life that Mother's death had placed there. Preparing his meals, cleaning his home, lending the ease of her presence in the evenings as they read Harper's Weekly by lantern light. Listening to his tales of boyhood, soothing in their sameness yet charming as woven through Father's "young eyes."

Day-by-day she observed the regression, however slight. She watched his agility decline, each movement more calculated, his intellect increasingly muted and feeble. That fiery resolution she had so much admired – had so much *depended* upon – diminished like the afterglow of eventide.

Viola rose that morning like any other. After shuffling to the outhouse to do her business, she kindled a fire in the hearth. Still in her nightdress, she slipped on Father's Wellingtons and wandered out to the chicken coop to broadcast a couple handfuls of grain and gather eggs for breakfast. Strips of cured bacon were retrieved from the pantry shelf for frying and she began kneading dough for biscuits.

It was usually around this time the aroma of freshly brewed coffee grounds meandered its way upstairs to rouse Father from slumber, and Viola would smile at the familiar groan of floorboards as he ambled down the staircase to pat her shoulder and kiss her good morning. Viola remembered glancing up at the ceiling that morning, arms buried elbow-deep in a pastry bowl, anticipating those proverbial creeks and shuffles. And it wasn't until the biscuits were baked, the eggs scrambled, bacon warming on the hearth, that she mustered the courage to venture upstairs. Because something in her knew this day was not right, and somehow the quiet comfort of cooking breakfast would never be the same.

Most disturbing of all about Father's passing was that Viola believed she had failed him, that her love was not enough to heal him.

Viola immediately busied herself with final preparations.

She changed from her nightdress into Father's canvas waist overalls.

Thin shafts of sunlight burst through cracks in the eaves, and the scent of fresh hay lay heavy in the barn's rafters. She stared blankly for several minutes at all of Father's lovely tools hanging on the far wall of weathered pine – the hammers, rakes, several handsaws, an ax, auger, three anvils, a posthole digger. Little Gatto, the one-eyed mouser, sat atop Father's old horse tack, staring at her with cool indifference – no doubt irked that she had interrupted his game of swatting at divebombing swallows circling the eves protecting their young. For the first time in perhaps years, Viola looked past the wholeness of the vast structure and instead saw one long length of faded pink pine after another, all stacked together as individuals of the whole. Green moss had begun to creep about the north side of the roof, as though trying to reclaim the dead planks into the living, breathing trees they once were. Viola sighed. Father's barn coat hung on a horseshoe hook near the back door where he had placed it the evening prior.

Viola delved into a bin of pine boards and chose two dozen of the strongest and straightest. She leveled a pair of sawhorses on the dirt floor and began the tedious chore of measuring and sawing, fitting and readapting the boards to perfection before nailing them together as best she could. When the coffin was complete, she retrieved muslin and lye from Father's steamer trunk in the rafters and used his shovel to dig a deep grave next to Mother. It is where he belonged, after all. Where he yearned to be.

Viola picks a handful of wild daisies to place at the base of Mother's headstone. She pulls one free of the bunch and offers it to Father.

"I know you were never very big on flowers. I'm sure you'd rather have a swig from the old jelly jar here, wouldn't you Papa?" She pours a stream of Snowflake onto the base of the headstone, smiling a pang of envy for those with strong religion. *The innocent bliss of conviction. Such comfort. Such peace.*

Viola sighs and takes a seat between Mother and Father. Her gaze settles over the lake, still and near stagnant in the day's paling light. She closes her eyes as that eerie tingling at the nape of her neck starts up again, manifesting itself as yet another random stretch of obscure remembrance.

Nonna Isabelle's Passing.

Viola couldn't have been more than five or six years old. The house had been abuzz for most of a month, with distant family having traveled from afar to pay last respects. They came from Illinois, Kentucky, New York – one family as far away as Oklahoma. Every room in the house full of visitors. Even the barn a temporary residence, and the Hanson's down the road had put up several people as well. Mother's brothers and sisters, great aunts and uncles, cousins, long-time family friends, many of Father's kin. The women spent most of their time in the kitchen, cooking hordes of food for the hungry brood. Sour cabbage and venison sausage; pasta fagioli al forno; porcupine meatballs; shredded pork stew; spaghetti meatball supper; beggar's pudding with sack sauce; sweet potato and onion pie; minestrone soup and beet root pancakes, to name just a sampling. Father slaughtered a bull to keep all bellies full, which barely lasted through Mourning Time. The men remained in Father's study or in the yard around a bonfire, for the most part. Telling tales as they smoked cigars and drank whiskey from jelly jars, or straight from the bottle.

And though everyone had gathered for a sad occasion, the atmosphere was quite festive. Constant chatter and laughter filled each room. Children scrambled everywhere, many she had never met before, and most she would never see again, although over the years she many times overheard Mother sharing news received by letter, of this one making the journey to California; that one going off to war; another getting married or giving birth, and a couple passing on. Viola remembered some of the names and faces, and it always seemed peculiar that the eight-year-old boy she had run up and down the beach with during Nonna Isabelle's Mourning Time was actually old enough to go to war; or that ten-year-old Rebecca had married and given birth. Those faces were frozen in time, forever ingrained in her psyche as children.

The only room that remained off limits to casual activity during Mourning Time was the parlour. This is where Nonna Isabelle's body was kept. Someone – usually Mother, or an aunt or uncle - would occasionally enter the room and close the door behind them. Several times Viola tiptoed to that closed door and crouched to a sitting position, hugging her knees to her chest, listening. Muffled conversation. Long periods of silence. Many times crying, or out-and-out weeping.

One day, late in the afternoon, when most of the family was gathered outside to rest on the porch - sitting on rails; mingling around the fire; children squealing in the hay loft – Viola snuck inside the parlour and closed the door behind her. She stood there with her back against the door for what seemed an eternity, heart pounding.

Father and several of the men had removed all the furniture and placed it temporarily in one of the barn stalls. Candles were glowing everywhere – on the sills, many on the floor, and one tall and lovely red votive on the mantle, its steady flame reflecting off the hearth mirror. And in the center of the room lay Nonna Isabelle.

Viola walked slowly to the casket and ran her fingers over the polished mahogany. Fancy scrolls were carved into the four corners, but for the most part it was plain and smooth, like cool alabaster. The casket was set high, placed on sawhorses that Father had fashioned, and Mother had covered with a thick black shiny material. Viola retrieved a milking stool peeking from beneath the heavy folds and stepped up to peer inside.

Nonna Isabelle was dressed in her Sunday best, a lovely black silk skirt over a poofy crinoline, and a tight-laced bodice of shimmering forest green. Viola remembered Nonna wearing that outfit while she knelt next to her on the pew in church, as the congregation sang Amazing Grace. She always marveled at the wide burgundy sash at the waistline, and one time reached over to touch it. Nonna startled, then looked down at her with a warm smile, a wink.

Nonna lay on her back, dainty wrinkled hands folded across her chest. Beneath them was her little black bible, partially wrapped in a lacy white handkerchief. Her black onyx and ivory rosary was there too. A silver chain and cross, a present from Mother, rested squarely upon her chest, just above her hands. And her thick silver wedding band.

Mementoes were placed everywhere between her body and the white satin lining the inner casket. Sealed letters, addressed 'Isabelle,' 'Sister,' 'Loving Wife,' 'Dearest Aunt.' A raised postcard with lovely pink roses adorning the front, and a cancelled postmark dated 11 October 1874, from somewhere Viola couldn't quite make out. A tiny coin purse woven of gold human hair. A little rag doll, worn from years of love. A wilting white lily and one lone cockleshell. And tin types, some encased in fancy felt frames with bronze etchings, others just plain. There was one of a very young Nonno Elio sitting in a wing back chair, and Nonna Isabelle standing above, one hand resting on his shoulder. Their faces forever posed and stoic. There was one of her and Anthonie as well, although there was a bit of a blur across Anthonie's face, as he could never sit still for more than a minute or two.

Viola finally mustered the courage to look into Nonna's face and found, to her surprise, that she was somewhat relieved. Nonna's expression was slack, slight jowls a bit deeper defined than normal. Pale wrinkled cheeks plied with rouge and beginning to bruise around the edges. Long white hair arranged in that trademark braid, poised in one perfect rope strand over the top of her head. Viola found it quite curious, however, that two pennies rest atop her closed eyes.

Viola slowly extended her hand. She was shaking but couldn't stop herself. And just as she was about to touch one of the pennies, Mother's voice echoed from somewhere down the hall behind the closed door.

"Viola!"

Viola jumped, jerking her hand - and the penny slid from Nonna Isabelle's eye to rest on her cheek. Her hand brushed against Nonna's clammy brow, and she yelped.

"Miele! Dove sei?"

She scrambled from the stool and crawled under the folds of material beneath the casket.

"Viola?"

The door opened, and she could see the hem of Mother's dress and the tips of her shoes in the open doorway. She held her breath. Mother lingered for just a few moments before gently closing the door again.

As Viola listened to Mother's footsteps retreat, she covered her face with her hands and sobbed.

V

12 May 1898

Viola has finished for the day, hanging Father's implements in the barn and heading toward the beach. She is barefoot, wearing camel canvas work pants with cuffs rolled past her shins. Oblong dirt stains are caked into the weave, knee to thigh, from unconsciously wiping her hands throughout the day. The sleeves of an ivory blouse are rolled past her elbows, showcasing the bramble scratches adorning her forearms and hands. A spatter of dandelion seeds, and tufts of floating cottonwood blossom are tousled about her unruly curls.

Another nightfall observes Viola as she winds down from her labours at water's edge, the billowy evening pallet of rose and lavender abundant with rumbling anticipation. She sighs and lies back on the warm sand, entranced by trapsing wisps of transparent cumulus which will soon be consumed by thunderclouds.

Your laughter ...
The magic of swaying as one
I'll remember you long after, my love
The moonlight slips into dawn

Viola bolts upright and rolls onto her stomach, startled by the achingly sweet and sorrowful strain of a violin lilting from the bluff below her. She crawls on hands and knees to the crest of the bluff, hidden in seagrass, and peers below to find the source of the haunting melody.

There, next to a small campfire, is the stranger from The Market. He is turned away from her, offering his concerto to dusk. The song is so hauntingly beautiful it brings tears to her eyes.

I yearn for us to come together once more
To walk the beach, holding you close
Will I ever see you again, my love,
Or will you haunt my dreams instead?

Viola closes her eyes.

A warm August day. She and Joshua Iverson sitting next to one another on the dunes, panting and perspiring after an exhausting hour of tag and statues. Joshua leans over and places his lips firmly upon hers, then scrambles to his feet and howls full bore at the sun, beating his chest like a fierce warrior before rambling down the dune and diving into the water, fully clothed ...

Moonlight through the pines
Starshine on the lake

Will you and I be together once more, dear one
Or shall we leave this love behind?

Viola slowly crouches to her feet and slips quietly back to the house.

V

13 May 1898

The next morning begins a gentle mist of hazy cloud cover, so thick it seeps into Viola's pores and dampens her clothing. The chickens rouse a bit later than usual, if only by a few minutes, and set the momentum for a lazy day.

And the voices are insistent all day.

Viola tries in vain to ignore them, to shut the portal to her subconscious whilst tending daily chores. Feeding the chickens and collecting eggs. Cooking breakfast. Haying the cows and milking a pregnant Mucca. Checking bunny nibblings on the first shoots and weeding the garden in preparation for Third Planting. She had worked the ground to utter perfection the day before, but somehow this morning it didn't seem quite good enough.

Come visit us, Viola.

She scans the grounds for something out of the ordinary, some sort of satisfying, if outwardly mundane project to begin.

The lion's share of spring cleaning has already been completed. She had been bitten by the bug early, as the season had dawned prematurely. The sashes and panes have been scrubbed. The curtains and linens mended and fresh. The hayloft swept anew, and Father's tack rearranged - not once, but three times. On the surface order and purpose shone everywhere, yet the sly mental residue remained of tasks left undone.

Of course there is always the attic, but the thought of dragging the ladder to the second story and opening the trap amidst protesting creaks and fluttering paint chips and cobwebs sends a shiver of regret through Viola's heart.

Regret?

No, the attic can wait another day. It has waited, after all, for twelve years, so what is another in the vast scheme of days?

Lunch for Viola is a thick slice of apple pie and a tall glass of fresh cream.

Afterwards, Viola settles on her oils, as she seems to do her best work in times of angst. She finds great comfort in the ritual of preparation. Setting up the easel on the porch next to the rocker. Opening Mother's old sewing box and sorting through cylinders of color. Arranging the appropriate glob of each in its place on the spattered pallet. Organizing the brushes and welcoming a fresh, blank canvas, soon to be the recipient of yet another little piece of her soul – a melancholy mixture of grief and beauty, at times bordering bittersweet rapture, sorrowful and obscure.

Viola stares at the blank canvas, as she always does when beginning a new project, waiting for that wash of epiphany to take on a life of its own. But this time she stares herself into distraction, and her wandering eyes land on the eaves of the barn instead. She is in serious need of repair, as many of the boards suffer from dry rot, and the tin roof has long since rusted and begun to rot through in several places. Efforts should be concentrated there. The structure most certainly cannot withstand many future seasons of rain and thick snow, as all the hay and alfalfa crop stored there will mold and fester.

Viola chooses one of the fatter brushes and dips it into blue and yellow. She dabbles and fans the brush back and forth to mix the colors until all the horsehairs are saturated green, then swipes a deep gash across the virgin canvas. Not quite right. How about a tad more yellow? A dash of black - a flourish of horizontal strokes - left to middle and back again - and she wonders what in the hell this is supposed to be, and *who in the hell do I think I am anyway, calling myself an artist?*

"Oh, this won't do at all," she mutters aloud, "questo è orribile."

Viola places the brush into a canning jar of turpentine and leans back on the stool, folding her arms across her chest and staring at the strokes of muddied brown on the injured canvas.

Come visit us, Viola.

She decides the barn still needs cleaning. Several hours pass as she works Father's splintered rake to gather barely soiled bedding hay from stalls, dumping it from the wheelbarrow to a compost pile out back. That complete, a dozen fresh bales are thrown from the rafters and strewn about, and through the rest of the afternoon they are relentless.

Please Viola...

As Viola returns the rake to its resting place, a thick sliver buries deep into her thumb. She tries to set it free by squeezing, and a crimson pebble pops from the tiny wound.

Viola pulleys a pail of water from the well and empties it into the kitchen basin. She submerges both hands, and with a sisal brush scrubs at the dirt beneath her nails and the creases of her fingers. Twice she brushes against the sliver, launching her thumb into a tight throb. The water turns pale pink as she scrubs and scrubs, until her hands themselves are prunish and raw. The skin burns.

Come visit us.

Viola sighs. She dries her hands on her shirt as she ascends the staircase to change clothing.

The cemetery is damp and wild, shaded by an overgrown canopy of oak branches and hanging moss. Viola ducks low and brushes them from her face in passing. Many of these trees were mere saplings when the cemetery's first inhabitants were lain here over 150 years ago. Hundreds of headstones offer a brief glimpse of long-forgotten souls.

Cyrus Weatherby
"Father and Friend to All Who Knew Him"
1801 – 1878

Suzanna Metsker
"Wife and Mother"
1820 – 1840

Beloved Baby Daughter
"The Good Lord's Cherub unto Eternity"
1774 – 1774

*Smallpox. Typhoid. Consumption. Suffocation. Influenza.
Measles. Crib Death. Heart Failure. Pneumonia.
Drowning. Hysteria. Childbirth. Murder.*

Shadows grow long and deep in this vast Place of The Dead. Stoic markers protrude from the earth as far as the eye can see. Elaborate slabs of marble, limestone, granite, with ornate carvings and cornices; others mere chunks of weathered maple or oak in the shape of a cross to mark their owner's final destination. Some of the epitaphs are so weathered they are barely decipherable.

And the distinction of class is present here, even in death. The Anderson Mausoleum to the immediate right of the entrance, almost obscene in its flagrant show of status and wealth. Pure emerald and white-veined marble obelisks, walls that are fifteen-feet high by at least thirty-feet long, with an elaborately-scrolled, wrought-iron entry gate and door of solid steel – the high-pitched screech of the hinges upon opening reminiscent of a screaming child. The Scottish family crest at the very top, guarded by an intimidating granite lion, one loping paw resting casually across the other as it appears to be daring interlopers to step within the parameter of its domain. Each time a new inhabitant is lain to rest, Enod Lictern travels from town in his rickety one-man wagon (quite resembling a Chinese rickshaw, but just a tad larger) and labouriously engraves the individual's name with hammer and chisel to the bottom of the list on a fancy scroll engraved into the side of the marble wall. Marlena Anderson, wife to the deceased lumber baron Carlton Anderson, was the last to join the list of dead. 2 November 1813 – 7 February 1879.

Viola's gaze lilts across the tops of tombstones that seem to ebb and flow like waves, one after the other, until it dumps into the back end of the cemetery. There, next to a splintered pine fence, is what residents call "the bone well." The bone well is essentially a hole in the ground with a manhole cover that houses the remains of Chinese who immigrated to The Thumb in the 1840's to build roads and work the farms. Most of them are gone now, having migrated to the UP to work the Iron Range and Huron Bay Railroad. There are no epitaphs to remember those lain here, as if they never existed at all.

Over here, Viola ...

Viola starts to tremble as she spins and swats at the back of her ear. She looks toward the entry of the cemetery and considers bolting for the main road, but then closes her eyes and breathes deeply several times.

Susan dearest, is that you? Oh, how I've wept for you!

I don't understand why I can't see him. He's left me! I can still hear him – smell him even - but my eyes! Oh Lord, my eyes! They are open, yet I cannot see...

Sweat begins to run in tiny rivulets down Viola's face to soak her lace collar. "You're the only one here," she chants, "only one here." Moisture is now dampening the creases in her bodice, and she can feel The Ambush creeping its way up her spine in cyclical electric zaps emanating from her tailbone.

*You son-of-a-bitch! I knew what you were up to all along!
You think you can run from me now, you're sorely
mistaken'! I couldn't wait to get down here to –*

"Hush!" Viola hisses. Lightheaded, she closes her eyes
again.

*Oh, please ma'am, have you seen my daughter? My darling
Sara – she's just a baby! Pleeeassse!*

*Don't go over there! He's evil! Longs to find another victim
and –*

Viola...

- please, my baby –

"NO!" she screams, cupping her hands over both ears as
she falls to her knees. "STOP IT! STOP IT! STOP IT!
"What do you want from me?!" she wails. *"Is this it?"* she
screams aloud, her voice echoing through the empty
afternoon. *"Is this all there is?!"*
She sighs and drops wearily to the ground, covering her
face.

*Am I meant to live amongst bittersweet memories so
ancient and detached they could belong to another - as
though relayed through casual conversation, local gossip,
folklore? Destined to live an isolated existence amongst
bumbling livestock, day-after-night-after-day, staring with
blank fortitude into meadows of sweet grass and the bosom
of woodland conceding to the swell of sand and tide?*

Viola lifts her face skyward.

Ah, these echoed whispers of long ago may haunt, but never torment, no. Rather a gentle comfort are they. For in solitude, one is never quite alone, as the voices and melancholy memories stay insanity. The unconditional love and comfort given, the caretaking which served as lifeblood nourishment to the soul. An ache once bourne so heart-heavy for everything lost, now a dull twinge, and only on rare occasion. That ache has retreated to quell the fire of that basic, yet essential desire to give and receive. That ache no longer hurtful, merely a vague numbness, having been courted so long by the pungent injustice of resignation.

Shadows begin to creep from the brush as daylight diminishes. The electrical zaps have transferred from her spine and are beginning to manifest themselves as the slightest tickle in her stomach – the place where The Ambush resides. She knows she must retreat now to stay the darkness. She looks toward the north end of the cemetery, and sighs.

"I'm so sorry," she whispers.

V

That night, Viola dreams.

The parlour is homey and comfortable, an easy place to relax after a day in the garden. Mother had decorated it in royal blue and tan. Four rawhide loungers, overstuffed and inviting, two of which huddle in front of the natural stone hearth. Picture frames are scattered about the mantle, images of Mother and Father in their first years of marriage, of her and Anthonie together in their youth. And one of her and Robert framed in faded pine. They are sitting on the porch of their home after its completion, young and peaceful, tired but happy. Robert in overalls, shirtless. She is sitting on the step above, embracing him from behind. Viola remembers it as though it were yesterday.

The parlour has remained in the same fashion for years, and every time she enters, she catches glimpse of Mother sitting in the chair next to the window, covered in blankets and resting; of Father nestled close to the fire, reading by lantern light. Though these memories are bittersweet and treasured, it is time to put them to rest. Time to rearrange the parlour.

Viola contemplates new arrangements. Perhaps move Mother's lounger from beneath the window and place it next to the other two by the hearth. And the fourth lounger presently resting in the corner across the room would look right fine there as well. Bring them all together in a half-moon arc in front of the fire. She nods with satisfaction and begins to push her weight against the chair – but is taken aback by a sudden, albeit mild tingling sensation in her mouth. She stops.

Viola's tongue runs across her teeth, and to her utter dismay, they "shift." She reaches into her mouth with both hands - frantic fingers trembling - and is horrified to discover her teeth are crumbling. Agony radiates through her sinus cavity and explodes into a horrific throb of unbearable pressure. She stumbles, hyperventilating and struggling not to pass out from the pain. Something slimy and bulbous begins to crawl from her stomach into her esophagus and her fingers become entangled in a tattered, fleshy cord spilling into her mouth. The meat of the cord extends into the core of her gut – so incredibly deep it feels as though it is connected to her bowels - and the sickening tug of the connection leaves her yearning to vomit or faint or die ...

As Viola despairs in the realization that her passageway is closing, she panics and yanks – and with a vulgar, squishy POP! a bloody mass of pulpy flesh, bile and teeth plops out of her mouth, into her open palms.

Viola screams.

V

14 May 1898

The next morning, Viola decides it is time to paint the barn.

Father had told her many a time about the barn raising back when he was a boy, when Nonno and all his old cronies from town spent three days putting her up, then having a celebration that lasted another two days on top of that. Viola always thought of her as charming and quaint but studying her from an entirely objective perspective certainly transformed her into an impending liability.

From her perch on the front porch, staring at the barn, Viola remembers the days she worked with Father in the garden, near the foreboding shadows of the structure.

She had been Father's garden sprite as long as she could remember, and drew comfort working by his side. Sometimes she used his rake and hoe to shape the moist earth; other times she used bare hands, digging deep and encouraging the dirt to embed itself beneath her nails before letting it crumble between her fingers and fall away. Sometimes she would take a handful of that luscious black gold and bring it to her nose, close her eyes and breathe deeply - and once, when she opened them, she caught Father watching. He just nodded and smiled. *"Kindred spirits,"* he whispered with a wink, handing her a bunch of leeks he had just pulled from the ground.

And she had been Father's student, as well. She soaked up his wisdom of the earth and planting, especially his passion for astronomy and the importance of charting the seasons of stars. They spent many an evening on the bluff together after dusk, lying flat on their backs gazing at the night sky as Father taught her to map the heavens. The myths behind Little Bear, Ursa Minor, Lupus the Wolf and Ophiuchus, Serpent Bearer.

She will never forget the time Father snuck into her room in the middle of a moonless night, rousing her from deep slumber and oh! so excited! His eyes sparkling wide with glee as he took her hand and guided her outside – him in his trap-door long johns, and she in her pale pink nightgown as they stole onto the bluff.

"Look!" he exclaimed, his childlike wonder filling her with joy. "Right there! Do you see her?"

Father bent down behind her on one knee, and with his large, warm hand directed her slender arm to the ebony sky, gently positioning her index finger as a pointer. Together they traced the heavens.

"Andromeda," he whispered. "Lady of Heavens. As legend has it, my dear one, Queen Andromeda's mother,

Cassiopeia of Ethiopia, offended the Nereid sea nymphs by boasting that her daughter was more beautiful than they, so in revenge, Poseidon sent a sea monster to devastate the Ethiopian kingdom. Since only the sacrifice of Andromeda would appease the Gods, she was chained to a rock and left to be devoured by the sea monster, Cetus."

"Oh no!" Viola shrieked, covering her mouth.

"Ah, don't despair! Along comes Perseus – Slayer of Monsters! He beheaded the Gordon Medusa and cast the monster into stone! Perseus saved Andromeda and they married."

"Yay!" Viola squealed, clapping.

"Upon her death, Athena, the ancient Greek Goddess of wisdom and warfare - the great protectress – set Andromeda into the sky as a constellation, an esteemed honor, so she may live unto eternity for all to see."

And the brilliance of lovely Andromeda unexpectedly popped from the deep coal pallet of night.

"Can you see her, mi amore?"

Viola could see her clearly, as though the mighty muse shone herself to only the two of them.

"Mighty Andromeda," she whispered, smiling.

"Ah, but Andromeda has nothing on you, my love! You are the fairest maiden of all!" Father planted a kiss atop her head. "Uh oh – we better watch out for sea monsters!"

She giggled frantically and threw her arms around Father's neck. Never had she experienced such magic – such an intense awareness of being alive – and all at once she was struck by a vision of past colliding with future; surrendering to the woman she would become, open to a vast universe of possibilities.

Viola had always considered that moment atop the bluff with Father as one of several distinct turning points in her life. Recounted with a soulful touch of mourning for the beginning of the end of innocence.

And somehow, although she can't quite remember exactly how or when, their beloved old barn had been dubbed "Mighty Andromeda," a moniker shortened over the years to "Sweet Andie," and then finally, just plain "Andie."

The bell attached to the coiled spring on the screen door jangles furiously as Viola enters the Bay Port Mercantile & Emporium.

Sun shone through one of the many tall, 16-box window grilles in the large cabin-style building, sending dust modes spiraling in passing. The Mercantile had been constructed of red maple in 1825 when there were barely any settlers in The Thumb, and though it was starting to show wear - both inside and out - the building remained solid. The subtle scent of mildew mingled with smoky white pine and eastern hemlock that seeped into the walls from the pot belly stove in the corner, which burned all day and night during the cold Michigan winters along The Huron.

The Mercantile was a sight to behold. No space was left empty, as items were stacked along the counters and floor-to-ceiling shelves – even hanging from the ceiling itself. Spices and teas lined the main counter. Barrels of hard candies – mint, butterscotch, cinnamon – lined up beneath glass display cases filled with precious stones, bowie knives, flasks, tobacco, guns, cartridges and shells. Washboards, lanterns, pots, pans and colanders hung from large iron hooks screwed into the ceiling joists. Shelves held tinctures, medicines, rose water, bear grease and other beauty products. Maple syrup, coffee and graniteware boilers, pickling vinegar, jellies, storage canisters. Sacks of sugar, flour and salt lay stacked on the floor next to flats of hickory and oak slats used for smoking. And toward the back were the building supplies, stove polish, denim pants and work boots, collars and men's hats, bolts of cloth and baskets full of needles, yarn and thread.

Viola jumped at a loud, repetitive banging coming from behind the front counter. A seventy-year-old man with an eclectic shock of snowy hair, circular spectacles and a black merchant's apron is banging on the cash register.

"Hello there, Mr. Fagan."

Willy Fagan scowls over the spectacles balanced precariously atop the bridge of his nose. His expression quickly softens to that of Welcoming Merchant, with just a hint of smirk.

"Oh, good day, Mrs. Thompson…

Viola skirts around a display of *"Newly Arrived Egg Beaters from England!"* positioned strategically next to the counter, and takes mental note of Willy's savvy marketing placement, as only three remain in the case.

"I'll be needing some paint and brushes today, Mr. Fagan."

Willy crosses his arms over his chest and strokes his pock-marked chin as he stares at the ceiling.

"Hmmm."

Viola sighs and fights the urge to roll her eyes like Mother used to. Willy Fagan: *'If-There's-Anything-To-Know-About-Anyone-Or-Anything-I'm-Your-Man-Fagan.'* Reveler of gossip, obsessive in his quest to dissect and broadcast the goings-on of everyone in town – especially the goings-on (or lack thereof) of someone like The Old Hermit Widow on Giordano Bluff.

Taking on a little project, are we Mrs. Thompson?"

Viola stares at him.

"I have Carl tied to a post out front and I don't want to leave him too long."

Willy grunts and points to Aisle Ten, dismissing her.

Viola makes her way around another display, this one of tin and copper watering cans, spades, forks, garden dibbles and cotton gloves. She is aware of Willy's beady eyes burning two tiny divots between her shoulder blades and can feel the blush of anger rising from her chest and neck to splotch her cheeks. A trait that forever frustrates. Whenever she becomes angry or unsettled, blotches of red appear, giving her away. She would be a horrible poker player.

Viola recalls their falling out shortly after Father's death. Willy had made it his personal mission to snoop and pry into every detail of his passing, just as with Mother and Robert. Viola cherishes family – considers personal affairs sacred - and this little weasel's apparent glee as town crier of her grief enraged her. She'd confronted him at The Market one day in July, and her ravings made her a hero in certain circles. But mostly they just offered townsfolk another clever adjective to interject in their whisperings. Old. Widow. Hermit. *Crazy.*

Who cares if Mrs. Hanford and Shelly Myer sit at the bakery all abuzz after she walks by? Who cares if the children in town cover hushed giggles, pointing at The Old Widow on her way to the fish market? Who cares if all the older women still look at her – will always look at her – with sympathetic eyes, while others keep extra watchful eyes on their husbands in her presence?

None of these people really know her. Some of them – some of the older ones – knew her in youth, attending church or choir practice and quilting circles with Mother. Others remember the charming young tomboy helping Father herd cattle to town on Market Day in a grey woolen cap, waistcoat, and breeches. *"Can't have you fussin' 'round in all that lace and linen doing farm work!"* he would say. Mother would frown for a second or two, then just shake her head in resignation.

Viola casually saunters amongst the aisles, letting her eyes fall upon items whilst surveying the perpetual list in her head. *Do you need steel wool for the pots? No – can still get a bit of distance from the old ones. A new veggie peeler? No – the paring knife is doing just fine. More lids for the canning jars? That would be a yes.* She blew a dozen during the last batch of kraut as she started too late, her mind weary and wandering after a full day of harvest. Viola grabs a clump of 24 lids wrapped in twine and places them in her grapevine basket. *These are not inexpensive. Must be more careful.*

The bell above the door seems to jangle nonstop as townsfolk enter the mercantile. Saturday is always a busy time here. Viola tries not to look up, as she will inevitably see someone she knows. She is not one for small talk and would lest not engage in such mindless dribble. Or even worse, lock eyes with someone who will turn to the person next to them and whisper tepid twists of gossip behind a cupped hand, as though she's not standing right there and hasn't a clue what they're doing.

Viola continues to scan the items with eyes that have become unconscious, as her focus has turned to the snippets of conversation around her. "I really don't know if that bolt is large enough – we have an entire tablecloth and placemats to make…" (*cakes of beeswax for candles*) "How many pie tins do you think we need? Charles' side always eats us out of house and home, ugh…" (*raw chunks of lye for soap*) "I really don't care what that damn school of yours is askin' – I need your ass down in the field this week sinkin' posts, proper. Now take this up to the register …" *(liquid paraffin and hurricane lamp flutes)*.

Viola comes to Aisle 10. She sees a big sign boasting: NEW SHIPMENT FROM DETROIT! Several rows of that new ready mixed paint are stacked neatly on top of one another, and most of the red is gone already. Other colors are still relatively plentiful, such as white, charcoal black, brown ochre, yellow orpiment, blue azurite and green malachite. A display table next to the paint showcases information on how other more exotic colors can be created by mixing your own paint, like in the old days.

Viola remembers Mother hand-mixed colors from powdered plant pigments for her bedroom when she was a girl. Madder made red dyes; indigo made dark blue; saffron and pomegranate rind made yellow. Other colors were then mixed from these primary hues. As they painted her bedroom together, Mother told her how the native peoples filled abalone shells full of ground ochre and charcoal. They used pigments from various sources for paints, which included many different minerals, sap, dried plants and roots, berry juices and even blood – and binders of water, saliva, animal fats or urine. They then applied them with fingers, brushes, or by blowing them through hollow bones.

Viola grabs four buckets of red, two in each hand, and carries them to the counter. She goes back for three more – plenty for Carl to carry in one trip – and stacks them neatly in front of Willy, who squints at her from behind his spectacles.

"Big project, I see."

Viola quells a fleeting compulsion to haul off and slap him. Without acknowledging his inquiry, she makes a trip outside and loads the first four buckets into Carl's pannier, then comes in to grab the last three and heads for the door without looking back.

"If you would be so kind as to place this purchase on my account," she says, letting the door slam shut behind her.

Four

SAMUEL

15 May 1898

Viola is on a ladder in canvas work pants and one of Father's old cotton nightshirts. Her long black hair cascades to her waist when free, but today is pulled into a loose bun. Scattered wisps of silver, like shining silk, are woven throughout, heaviest at her temples. Red paint spatters are speckled about her hair, face, and forearms.

From her perch atop the ladder, Viola can see the vast expanse of rolling hills as they meld into the beach and The Great Huron. The wind is moderate today, and gulls ride the stream above the barn. She marvels at the purity of their white breasts, the freedom and agility of their flight.

Movement catches Viola's eye toward the east, toward town. A little speck of a person on the beach, headed west. Another solitary traveler coming from the ferry, perhaps. Many of them traverse this length of beach on their way to the train station at Bern Junction. The speck disappears amidst the trees and then reappears, seeming to take a curve toward the south in the direction of the homestead.

Viola shifts her focus back to the task at hand. She dips

her brush back into the paint bucket she has propped on one of the windowsills and assaults faded pink boards with a new slash of red. As she prepares to dip the brush again, her attention is once more drawn away toward the beach path. The stranger, a man, is making his way toward the house. He is at the 'Y' in the path when he spies her atop the ladder and waves. As he draws closer, she sees it's the violin player. He seems to have a slight limp.

"Good day," he bids in greeting, flashing a smile that is unexpectedly warm and approachable.

"Good day," she returns, smiling cautiously.

The stranger shifts the load of his haversack from his shoulder and sighs, stretching. "Just came from the ferry a couple days ago," he announces, slipping off his hat to wipe his brow. Atop his head lay a mane of wavy charcoal grey, which he promptly covers again with the hat in a seesaw rocking motion. "On my way to the gypsum plant in National City. Fella on the vessel said to head east down the beach here and I'll come to it."

Viola smiles and looks north. "True, you'll come to it eventually," she says, "but certainly not before dusk. You have quite a walk ahead of you, a good three to four days."

He flashes that smile at her again. Aside from the fact that she's seen him before, something in the way about him seems oddly familiar. Maybe the tilt of his head, or the way one side of his moustache curls up higher than the other as he smiles. Something she can't quite put her finger on.

"Oh, that's okay, ma'am. I've done my share of walkin' over the years."

Viola likes the way he said *'ma'am.'* Not as a moniker reserved for those of elderly status, rather a show of respect, laced with an ever-so-subtle hint of flirtation. This man is different from those she is accustomed to, the slow-witted boorish sort roaming the streets of Bay Port as though all bourne of the same mother. *This* man has an earthy charisma about him. A quality Robert possessed. One which made him stand out from the others.

"Have any recommendations on a good place to stay for the night? Cheap is good, free is better."

And Viola Thompson, widow of Robert Joseph Thompson, orphan of Antonello Giordano and Laura Romano-Giordano, sister of Anthonie, surprises herself by saying, "Well, as a matter of fact, I do."

That night, healthy slumber eludes Viola.

She sleeps for an hour or so before rustling awake, certain there is someone standing in the doorway, then tiptoes to gaze out the window toward the barn to see if the glow of the lantern still shines like a lonely lighthouse beacon in the night.

Viola has absolutely no idea what came over her. *A brain fart*, as Anthonie used to say when they were children. That was it, had to be. There is no other logical explanation.

The stranger had followed her back up the path to the house, speaking in that soothing, low baritone all the way. He was Samuel Elliott, hailing from the North and just recently up from Detroit and traveling through these parts for work, and he was honored to make her acquaintance and sure grateful for her hospitality. Viola had been certain to let him know it was more a matter of being cordial, than hospitable. Hospitality just had too cozy a ring to it for her liking.

Just as she is about to slip back under the covers, a melancholy chord flows into the silent night, drawing Viola back to the window like a siren's call. Samuel is playing the same concerto from the beach, so utterly beautiful and haunting it stirs her to tears. She goes back to bed and listens until she finally drifts off again.

The last time she awoke, at 2:02 AM, the barn was finally dark.

V

16 May 1898

Henry crows his welcome to dawn at 4:55 AM. Viola rolls over and places a pillow on her head to drown him out. She had fallen back to sleep again sometime after 3:00 AM, but she is an eight-hour-a-night girl, and without it, quite a grump.

Viola dangles her feet over the side of the bed as the first light of day filters into the room. The curtains flutter gently as Samuel's low mumblings float into the room on a mild breeze.

He is standing near the front meadow next the barn, one arm resting atop the fence as he pets Carl. The burro's head is plastered against the chicken wire as Samuel scratches first his ears, then his neck.

"Oh, you're a friendly one." He pulls a carrot from his pocket, taking a bite of it first before offering it to Carl. He is fully dressed in the same clothes from the prior evening, wearing his slouch hat and oilskin duster. His leather haversack is propped against the fence near his feet.

Viola hurries to the washbasin to scrub her teeth and face and brush night tangles from her hair. She pulls it back with a tortoiseshell clip, slips into her canvas dungarees and a fresh blouse, and tweaks her cheeks to blush them before walking downstairs to the porch, careful not to let the screen door slam behind her. Samuel stops petting Carl and flashes a brilliant greeting.

"Good morning!"

Carl is straining through the fence with his lips, trying to nibble at Samuel's duster.

"Good morning."

Samuel looks toward the beach as he takes off his hat to run a hand through his hair, a gesture she's certain he's performed at least a thousand times prior without even realizing it.

"Gettin' ready to head out," he tells her. "Just wanted to stick around for a bit to offer my gratitude. I really do appreciate your kindness."

"Did you sleep well?"

"Just fine."

Viola's arms are crossed in front of her. She looks down at her bare toes and brushes one foot against the faded pine.

"Well, thanks again. I'll be headin' off to National City then." Samuel picks up his pack and slings it over his left shoulder as he reaches through the fence to give Carl one last scratch. He moves toward the trail and turns to wave. Viola waves back, biting her lower lip, and almost can't believe what she's about to do.

"Hey Samuel -"

He stops walking and turns.

"Ma'am?"

"I was about to put some breakfast on the hearth. Why

don't you stick around a while. That's quite a walk to undertake on an empty stomach."

Samuel pauses. She wonders if he's contemplating under which category this offer is made – cordial or hospitable. He smiles finally, stirring a little flutter in her chest.

"That would be right fine," he tells her, heading back toward the house.

𝒱

Samuel stays outside while Viola sets about the task of cooking breakfast. Egg skillet, frying pan for bacon, the kettle to boil water for coffee and oatmeal. Robert always loved her oatmeal, smothered in fresh cream and butter with a scoop of brown sugar. Sometimes, when they were in season, she'd even toss in a handful of blueberries. Just as the water is about to boil over, heavy footsteps sound upon the porch, followed by a light wrap on the screen door.

"Yes?"

Samuel ducks just slightly to clear the entryway. He is holding his hat before him, chest-level, twirling it at the brim.

"I was just wonderin' if you needed any help."

He is tall, very tall, and Viola notices the first three buttons of his shirt are unfastened, exposing curly grey hair.

"Oh no, I've got it pretty much handled here. Almost done, really. Oh - wait a minute! You could go out and gather some eggs from the girls, if you don't mind."

Samuel nods. "Done." he says with a smile.

Viola peeks through the window to watch him walk toward the chicken coop. Yes, there definitely is a bit of a limp there. Nothing drastic or constant even, real subtle. He

64

moves in such long graceful strides – *fluid* is the word that comes to mind – that it's rather difficult to detect. A few moments later he returns with a cache of eggs tucked into his hat.

"Where should I put 'em?"

"Over there on the block is fine."

Samuel carefully places half a dozen eggs, one by one, in a neat row in the center of the butcher block.

"There's a mug of coffee over there for you." She gestures her head toward the counter while stirring oat flakes into a large pot.

"Oh, thank you kindly, ma'am." Nothing like a good cup of coffee to start the mornin' right. Anything else?"

"No, I'm just about finished. Why don't you go make yourself comfortable. I'll bring it out when it's done. We can eat on the porch."

We. There you go again, Viola.

Viola continues to watch him through the window as she scrambles the eggs. Samuel is strolling about the yard, taking everything in; one hand holding the mug, the other tucked in the front pocket of his dungarees. He surveys the cows grazing in the pasture; seems amused by the chickens as they scratch and peck for bugs; and stops to absentmindedly pet Carl as he once again considers the barn, the hayloft in particular.

Viola sighs and carries two steaming plates full of breakfast to the porch.

"You have a mighty fine place here."

Samuel has finished his first helping and is well into his second. Viola marvels at how much he can put away, just like Robert used to. Sign of an active man. She could walk through town on Market Day and instantly pick out the bankers and lawyers and City Hall Fat Cats, the ones who sat behind desks all day with idle lives of leisure.

Samuel gazes into the pasture. "Have anyone here to help you out? Sure is a lot of land for one person."

"Nope. Just me. I manage though."

They finish the rest of their breakfast in a comfortable silence. Viola watches him lift the spoon to his lips and then chew slowly, as though savoring every bite. His salt-and-pepper mustache twitches back and forth and he is shaking his head slowly as he sits back in his chair and groans with satisfaction, patting his stomach.

"My goodness, Ms. Thompson, you are one *fine* cook. I honestly can't remember the last time I had a bonified home-cooked meal. Many thanks."

"You're quite welcome."

Viola takes their empty plates into the house and returns with the coffee kettle. He holds out his mug. She observes his large hands and long, lovely fingers, imagines them working the strings of his violin. She fills her own mug and sets the kettle on the porch between them.

"I have a proposition for you," he says.

"Oh? And would that be of a cordial or hospitable nature?"

Samuel throws his head back and has a hearty laugh at her playful quip. "Well, let's just say it would be mutually beneficial," he chuckles.

Viola is curious and sits down to sip her coffee, indicating she is ready to listen.

"Your barn there –"

"Andie."

"Beg pardon?"

"Andie. Her name is Andie."

He chuckles. "Okay, yes, Andie! I see you've started to paint Ole' Andie on your own, and though I have no doubt you're of the will to take on this kind of project, Ms. Thompson, it could take a long time. She's in pretty bad shape there. I'd say she's, what, at least seventy, eighty years old?" Viola nods. "Boards full of dry rot, several already fallin' through. Hasn't been painted in Lord knows how long. It's good you've got started 'cause you let Andie go too many more years like that, and you'll find yourself needing to replace the whole darned thing."

Viola nods again and looks into her mug.

"Yes, well, she is in disrepair. No arguing that fact. So, what are you proposing?"

Samuel walks down the stairs, motioning her to follow. "Well, this is the type of thing I do. I could be your hand. All I'd ask in return is one good meal a day and a place to rest my head."

Viola always thought of Andie as charming and quaint, but studying her from Samuel's perspective reminded her the structure is a looming burden.

She looks into her mug again and picks out a little no-seeum. "How long do you think it would take?"

Samuel squints, calculating dimensions more seriously. "Well, depending on how soon we could obtain more supplies, and assuming the weather holds, I'd say a good thirty to forty days, give or take a few."

Viola looks back into her coffee cup, recognizing what Samuel says may likely be true. She has the will, but perhaps not the endurance to both tend to the stead and finish painting before the first snow.

"What about National City?"

"It ain't goin' nowhere. I got nothin' but time."

Viola stares at the barn, then Samuel, and again finds herself in utter disbelief.

"Okay." She nods. "I'll check on materials at The Mercantile in town this afternoon."

Viola turns back toward the house. A gentle breeze has kicked up, rustling the porch chimes. "I'll get some more blankets for you," she says without looking back, "and lunch will be at noon."

V

17 May 1898

Samuel begins work on the barn, and she leaves him alone, for the most part. Tells him when lunch or supper is ready. He eats alone on the porch most of the time while she eats inside at the table. They are cordial, and she finds herself wondering about him. Wondering where he came from. Of his time in the Great War – she's assuming he was in the war, as he's the right age for it. If he's ever been married, or if he's a father. Where he will go after National City, and why.

Every night she looks forward to hearing his violin. When he finally blows out Father's lantern, usually sometime between 11:00 PM and midnight, she turns out her light and goes to sleep.

One night her curiosity gets the best of her, and she decides to go up to the loft just before dusk to deliver more blankets.

"Hellooo," she calls from below. She begins ascending the staircase and when she gets to the top, he is standing there looking away from her, violin cradled below his chin. He wears his dungarees, but no shirt. His shoulders and biceps are in fiddlers' stance, gleaming and firm.

"Oh I'm so sorry!" she says, blushing and turning away. "I didn't mean to disturb you – I just thought you could use more blankets."

"Sorry ma'am," he says.

She can hear him fumbling for his shirt and waits a few moments before turning back around. He's standing there facing her now. His shirt is on, but the top four buttons are not fastened. She tries not to look at him, as she can barely take her eyes away from his chest. *I know what that feels like*, she chuckles to herself.

"Here you go," she says, handing him the blankets.

"Very kind of you, Viola, thank you."

Viola nods and smiles, quickly dashing back down the stairs.

Five

Companions

24 May 1898

On the dawn of the seventh day after Samuel's arrival, with the renovation project in full swing, it begins to rain. A warm, driving rain that turns hard-packed soil of the past month into trickling arteries and muddy rivers. Long, rolling rumbles of thunder echo off the muggy hills before dissipating over Lake Huron.

Viola opens the top bureau drawer, rummaging through lace doilies, a pair of white gloves, several handkerchiefs, until she finds what she is looking for. A jar of pink rouge, lip colour, a couple bottles of lavender and rose scented au de toilet. She chooses the rose and shuts the drawer again, feeling girlish. A flush has risen to her cheeks.

She peers out the bedroom window. Samuel is down by the corral next to the barn, petting Carl. Rain drips from his brown slouch hat down the back of his shirt, but he doesn't seem to mind.

Viola bends over the dressing table and peers into the

mirror. Surely these fading hazel eyes surrounded by crow's feet belong to another, the long wispy strands of grey at her temples a grievous mistake. She squints and draws closer, looking deeper. That sixteen-year-old girl is in there too, somewhere, has always been there. Just waiting.

Viola unscrews the lid to the jar of lip stain, a light shade of honey-gold. She spreads it across her lips with her pinky, bringing them together to even out the color. Next a puff or two of rouge to accent her cheekbones, and finally a couple dabs of rose water behind her ears, on her wrists, one last down the crest of her bosom.

She looks at herself in the mirror, suddenly feeling quite foolish. *What are you doing?!* She grabs a handkerchief and brings it up to her cheek. After staring at herself for a good 30 seconds, she decides to let it stay and walks downstairs to make a pot of coffee.

By midday they are still sitting on the porch together, oblivious of the pouring rain and unfinished chores.

Samuel speaks of his life as though a test for some task not yet encountered. Harvest hand in Missouri. Wagon train driver throughout the West. Skinning mules and selling buffalo meat in Nevada. Panning for gold in the Snake River Canyon. Many souls have crossed his path over these years, some of them long remembered, some not, and Viola wonders how many of those faces were young and obliging, how many whispered their tales to *him* in the night.

"So where are you headed after National City?"

Samuel starts to slowly rock, stretching his muscular legs in front of him. His feet are bare, and he wiggles his long, elegant toes.

"Well, eventually the UP. There's another big cut goin' on right now. Hard work, but you get paid right fine, plus three square meals. But my dream is to go West again, Wyoming, Montana maybe. After that, who knows? Haven't gotten quite that far yet."

The rain is slamming against the roof, sliding down the eves and shooting through the soffits where it sluices into the earth and flows in turbulent muddied rivers down slope, toward the lake.

"More coffee?"

"Sure, thank you."

Samuel holds his cup in front of him as Viola carefully fills it to the brim. His hands nearly engulf the white porcelain. He looks up, eyes smiling in appreciation.

"What about you, Viola Thompson? What events in your life find you alone on this homestead?"

Viola refills her own cup and sighs, somewhat surprised by the directness of his inquiry.

"My," she says finally. "That, my friend, is a long story."

"That may be so," he says, "but looks like we have nothin' but time." Another rumble echoes through the hillsides.

And what are the events, exactly, that have brought you to this point in your life, Viola Thompson? How does one summarize a lifetime into a manageable paragraph? A widow, or spinster by many accounts. The myths surrounding your past have been regurgitated on so many lips over the years, the story rewritten at least a dozen times. Viola Thompson, a woman of mystery. Imagine that!

"I'm afraid my story isn't all that interesting."

"Oh, I highly doubt that. Something tells me you have

quite a tale to tell."

Viola looks away, into the rain. Carl is standing just inside the barn, watching them.

"Perhaps another time."

Samuel stares at her for several moments before dropping his gaze.

"Well then," he says, "how 'bout I help you with those potatoes you brought up from the cellar this mornin'?"

She nods, and Samuel follows her into the house.

"So, quid pro quo, Samuel Elliot. Who are you?"

They stand side-by-side in front of the double-wide counter basin, peeling potatoes. Two oil lamps cast their glow in the afternoon gloom. She is using her paring knife and Samuel his own pocketknife, slowly and expertly peeling the skins. She notices the graceful movement of his fingers and hands as he holds a potato in one, works the knife with the other. His hands are large and thick, his agility a surprise.

"Whad'ya wanna know?"

"Where are you from? That's always a good place to start."

Samuel chuckles. "Oh, from a little bit of everywhere, I suppose. The North, the South, Mexico. Down the banks of the Amazon and further still. A lil' bit of my soul residue rests in the Himalayan Mountains of Tibet as well. More than a bit, actually."

"Hmmm. An enigma, you might say." She finishes a potato and places it into a bucket on the floor between them.

He chuckles. "Oh, nothing too mysterious - just livin'

life, I suppose. Leave a bit of myself wherever I go." He reaches into the basin with one of his large, lovely hands and begins his expert handiwork on another.

"Where were you born?"

"Red Wing, about fifty miles southeast of Minneapolis on the banks of the Mississippi. Parents had a farm there, cows and pigs mainly."

Viola looks out the window. Mucca is standing just inside the barn, keeping dry. Her jowls work rhythmically as she chews cud.

"So, you're a farm boy."

"Used to be."

"How did you end up in all those other exotic places?"

Samuel smiles, contemplating his hands. Viola suddenly feels foolish, but decides his grin is one of amusement, rather than patronizing. He's enjoying the attention.

"After four years in The War, guess I had what they call 'a fallin' out with identity.' Didn't know who I was, didn't really fit in anywhere. I completed the mission my country had set before me, but didn't believe in the cause anymore. Didn't think it was all worth it."

"Well how could you say it wasn't worth it – freeing the slaves, I mean? Surely you don't believe in slavery?"

Samuel pauses, his face shadowed in lantern light. "Is that what you think The War was really about, Viola? Freein' slaves?"

"Well of course Samuel, everyone knows that. You're telling me it's not true?"

Samuel looks back down at the potato in his hands. "It was about power and money, plain and simple. With the Southern states seceding, the Union was losin' massive funds in cotton and other exports. And with the Union wantin' the South to stop slavery, the South was losin' their industry in the flesh trade. There may have been noble intensions in there as well – I keep tellin' myself as much - but what it all boils down to, what everythin' boils down to, is power and money."

Viola places another potato in the bucket, and they work in silence for a spell. The distant patter of rain and the grandfather clock in the hallway accentuate the quiet.

"So where did you go after The War?"

"Up north to check on my folks in Minnesota, then headed south, just about as far south as you can go. Guess that was my way of rebellin' against the Union, try and forget what I'd done. Make amends in some twisted way by secedin' from the entire country. I hooked up with a wagon train in San Antonio down to Mexico to work a rail line. After a couple years doing that, I headed to Peru."

Samuel pulls a handkerchief from his back pocket and wipes dirt from the blade of his knife.

"I traded my rifle for a dugout canoe in Chiclayo and floated down the Amazon until the rains swelled her into the jungle, into this village of native people who follow the old ways. The jungles down there are savage and unpredictable, like nothin' you've ever imagined. But the people are simple and gentle, livin' off the land and takin' only what they need. Their knowledge of plants and natural healing power is beyond anything of the western world. We think we're so advanced and civilized – *ha!* These people know the ways of the earth. They live within her realm, not try to dominate her."

The potato bucket is full. Viola reaches into the pantry for another.

"When the rains receded, I jumped back in my canoe and

floated to river's end. I abandoned the boat then and set out on foot. After close to a year, found my way to Tierra del Fuego, 'End of the Earth.' I was standing there on the beach where land meets water, starin' at the immense Strait of Magellan, and there was no doubt in my mind this is where it all began, or where it all ends, depending on one's perspective."

"Hmmm," she nods, retrieving another potato from the basin.

"There was a whaler full of Orientals docked in the Strait. I got friendly with a couple of 'em at the outpost one night. They couldn't speak a lick of English and I didn't know Chinese of course, but we connected all the same, jus' like with the natives. You communicate through these subtle nuances. Quite sublime, actually. Words jus' get in the way, complicate things. I convinced 'em to take me back with them. It was an easy decision on my part 'cause I was disconnected, without a home or country. No plan, no conviction, nothing holding me back. It jus' seemed like the right thing to do. I didn't realize at the time that I was runnin' away from demons."

The flame in one of the lanterns flickers, sending a flutter of shadow across Samuel's face.

"When we finally reached the port of Shanghai I was surprised; didn't know what to expect, really. The weather was calm and mild, like Georgia in the springtime. Beyond the bustling wharfs and city streets were these pockets of grand structures - pagoda's - surrounded by ancient blossoming apple trees, maples and willows. Fields of tulips and hyacinth everywhere – the air filled with sweetness. Heady. Maybe it was just being on a boat for two months made me a little stir crazy, but it was amazing Viola, so different from anythin' I'd ever encountered.

One night in this seedy lil' watering hole on the waterfront in Shanghai, I met another American named William Hartman from Mesa, Arizona. He was the first westerner I'd seen since I'd been there, and we gravitated toward one another like moths to a flame. Seein' him there, sitting across the room in a sea of Oriental faces, I realized how out of place I was in that world, how much I stood out amongst them. I would never be one of them – never could be – but they were gracious about lettin' me occupy a little space in their world, if only for a while."

Viola nods and reaches for another potato.

"It felt good to use my voice again. It was cracked and dry from underuse. We sat there like long lost brothers for hours, listenin' to the eerie whine of a pipa, takin' turns buying Maotai. He was a man of few words – or at least I thought at first – but I think he was just a bit rusty too. When he finally got going, he didn't stop.

He was rode hard and put away wet, this guy was. Weathered and grey, somewhere between forty and forty-five, I placed him. He'd been in China for ten or fifteen years; wasn't sure exactly 'cause he quit keeping track after the seventh. He'd just come from the Drepung Loseling Monastery in the hills on the northern outskirts of Lhasa, in India. Spoke of the light of dawn as it shone over craggy cliffs and outcroppings, like a moonscape full of spirits and longing. And it was somethin' in his eyes, a peace, a knowin' of ways far past his years that convinced me I had to travel there. Maybe I'd find what I was looking for in those ancient ways. Then again, maybe I was tirin' of rice and geishas and dim sum. Or maybe it was jus' the grain alcohol doin' its magic."

Viola smiles. "So, you went to the monastery?"

"Yup. William tore a page from his journal and sketched the vague idea of a map. Next day I headed out." Samuel places the last potato in the bucket. "Anything else?"

Viola pulls a bunch of carrots from the pantry that she harvested from the garden earlier in the day. "You can start chopping these, if you'd like, in little sections, like this." She places one of the carrots on her chopping block and cuts it into several small pieces.

"Was it worth it?" she asks him.

Samuel nods. "Oh, yes, it was worth it. It was everything I saw in William Hartman's eyes, and much more."

Samuel reaches for a carrot at the same time Viola is turning toward the potato bucket, knife in hand. The blade grazes his left wrist and draws blood.

"Oh my God!" she exclaims, searching frantically for a rag while blood begins to drip from his wrist and pool onto the butcher block.

"Oh my God – I'm so sorry, Samuel!"

Viola raps a rag around Samuel's wrist, tears pooling in her eyes.

"Now don't you worry about anythin' ma'am. It's a superficial wound. Looks much worse than it is."

"Well, that's good – because it looks like a pig was butchered on the block!

Samuel lifts his hand to look at the pool of blood that has seeped into the wood.

"Sorry, Viola – that one's not comin' out."

"What? Are you actually apologizing to me because I stabbed you?"

"Kind of sounds that way, doesn't it?" he says, eyes

twinkling.

They burst into laughter as Viola reaches for another rag to wrap around his wrist.

"Good Lord!" she exclaims. "Okay – you hold onto this and I'm going to fetch some alcohol and clean bandages. Be right back."

V

That evening after a supper of potato stew, coffee mugs are traded for jelly jars of Anthonie's Snowflake Whiskey on the porch.

Their conversation floats from one life experience to the next, as conversations often do. He tells her more of his travels in China and India, of the ten years he lived with the monks of the Himalaya. Viola, in turn, shares a history of Bay Port and her time as a young girl on the homestead. *So much has changed here*, she tells him, *since the days of my childhood.* The driving rain continues as though The Good Mother is making up for lost time.

Samuel has spoken to her in great generalities, for the most part. He is a touch elusive, which makes him all the more alluring. Viola is keenly interested in his time in the military, which he has mentioned in the abstract, and this intrigues her even more.

"What is your most vivid memory of The War?" she asks directly.

"Hmph," Samuel sighs, looking into his jelly jar at the amber liquid as he swishes it around in circles. "Well, there are many, Ms. Thompson, but I supposed the one that stands out most is the Battle at Corinth."

"Tell me about it."

Samuel looks up at her, then back into the jelly jar.

"Well, it's not the type of tale most gentleladies would be interested in hearing," he says, looking up at her.

"I'm not a gentlelady, so that shouldn't be a problem."

He throws his head back and roars. "You are a feisty one, Ms. Thompson! Okay; I'll tell you about my experiences at the Battle of Corinth. You stop me if anything gets too graphic."

She nods, eyes focused upon his face. He pauses for several minutes as though flipping through memories before proceeding.

"Well, the bellow of cannon fire started just after dawn," he begins. "First was this big, *BOOM!* then a screechin' *hissssssss!* headin' right toward camp. *Again! and again! and again!* they came, and I dropped my tin coffee mug, spillin' hot black grinds down the front of my uniform. Then the constant crack! of musket fire in the distance – like the 4th of July - and you could see the fine fog of gunpowder slowly approaching, even before the smell of it reached us."

He pauses to take a sip from the jelly jar.

"My tentmate was Walter Heslop, this Iowa kid with flamin' red hair and a bazillion freckles. Walter immediately flips out and bellows at the top of his lungs, *'MOVE YOUR ASS SAMUEL!'* He stumbles over the haversack next to the fire and falls right on top of the tent, flattening it like a pancake. *'WHERE'S MY RIFLE?! WHERE'S MY FUCKING RIFLE?!'* He's rummagin' through the rumpled tent and knocks over this bottle of corn whiskey we'd been passing back and forth the night before.

The ambush took us all by surprise. We thought they were gonna hit Corinth first. That's where we were headed - to Corinth as reinforcements. Never saw it comin'.

So, I bring my hands up to my face and they're shakin'. BAD. I reach for my rifle and rummage through my cartridge pouch while Walter is twirling around in circles, still searching for his weapon. *'WHERE'S YOUR RIFLE WALTER? FIND YOUR DAMN RIFLE!'* By this time these little grey and butternut speckles are swarming all over the farmland right below us, right toward us. They looked like a pissed off swarm of killer hornets on the move.

That's when I ran over to this decrepit outbuilding – a tiny barn or storage shed, something like that; I can't remember exactly – and Walter is still completely in the open, twirling in circles and goddamning himself on top of the tent and stumbling across the campfire. I'm crouching there beside the shed, trying to squeeze myself between it and this overgrown bramble, and all I can think of is how much I have to urinate."

Samuel looks over at Viola for the first time since beginning his story, to gauge her response to his intensity perhaps, or maybe his use of profanity. She nods, captivated.

"Walter lets loose this bloodcurdlin' scream just then, and though I'm terrified to take my eyes from the approachin' troops, I have no choice but to look over at him." Samuel closes his eyes. "Walter is on fire, fully engulfed from head to toe. When he knocked the whiskey bottle over it must of saturated his clothing, and when he stumbled across the open fire it ... he just ... *poof!*

He's flailin' around in blind circles, beatin' at his legs and chest trying to douse the flames. I remember thinkin' there's no way I can possibly reach him in time through all the musket fire around us now – there's no way I can make it there to put him out and hope to come through it myself. I became fixated on his flaming orange hair. Was that just the color of his hair? Or was his *hair* actually on fire now too? All those damned freckles of his - all over his face and arms - they seemed to be themselves aflame, little orange pinpoints of fire. But I had no choice. I had to go over there and help him.

I look from side-to-side," - Samuel rises from his chair, reenacting – "bring the rifle up in front of me, cradle it under my armpit. Just as I'm about to spring from my crouch this hand grabs my right shoulder, slammin' me back down to the ground. 'Don't be a fool, boy', I hear this voice bellow above the gunfire. I turn around and these searing grey eyes are staring back at me. They're bug-eyed and wiry, bloodshot but unyielding. Dust covers him from head to toe. His red hair – more red hair! – it's messy and wild, and his lips are crusty and cracked. A bloody bandage is wrapped aroun' one of his hands and a wreath of four bright yellow stars set on the shoulder of his blue uniform. Four stars means a General," he tells Viola, as an afterthought.

"General reaches for a revolver tucked to a harness under his left pant leg, aims it at Walter."

Viola gasps. Samuel is standing with his back to her now, staring toward the barn. A low rumble of thunder erupts somewhere in the night sky, and he waits until its echo melts away before continuing.

"I couldn't believe what I was seein'," he finally says. "The General was going to shoot Walter, gonna kill 'im. By pure instinct I lurch forward and knock him off balance. Instead of shooting Walter he brings the butt of the pistol down across my cheek, splittin' my lip wide open."

Samuel begins to slowly pace. One hand brushes against his lip.

"This knocks me silly for several seconds, givin' the General an opportunity to bring the pistol back up and aim it at Walter. I'm lyin' there in this half-conscious stupor and it's all happenin' in slow motion in front of me. He cocks the trigger, closes one eye, takes aim. Finger slowly squeezes down. The bullet releases from the chamber and I can see it floating in midair for just a second before it's lost in a fog of gunpowder. Walter's screaming stops abruptly, then the stench of burning flesh and whiskey hit me. I roll over to wretch. It could of just as easily been me."

Samuel walks to the rocker and drinks the last of his whiskey. He turns to Viola and smiles, motioning with the empty jar.

"Can I trouble you for a refill?"

"Yes, of course." She disappears into the house, returning with the bottle.

"Thank you, Viola."

The night air is charcoal black, punctuated by periodic flashes of lightning. Just inside the window behind her a lantern is burning. A lone moth beats itself desperately against the hurricane flute. Samuel takes another deep drink, visibly relaxing.

"Shall I continue?" he asks.

Viola nods.

"Well, before I can gather my wits about me, this horse comes charging up to us. The rider is a boy not much older than me. He jumps from the stag before it comes to a complete stop, makin' sure to hold the reins so the animal doesn't bolt away. Its eyes are bulging in terror, just as mine were, I imagine.

'General Sherman!' the boy yells. Without another word, Sherman and the boy jump back on the horse and gallop away, leaving me alone again.

By this time, a gritty carbon fog has completely obliterated everything around me. It was a wispy, whitish-grey fog, like down at the bog near my house when I was a boy, the bog where us boys found the body of a dead horse one time. It stings my eyes, and I can even taste it on my tongue. I fumble for my rifle and fit the bayonet on it.

Several pair of legs rush past me, jus' past the side of the shed. That's all I can see of 'em from down there on the ground, their legs. I can hear 'em shouting to one another and shootin' into the fog, and somewhere in the distance is this constant screaming and moaning. I can't tell if it's from one man or several different men, but it didn't make any difference at that point. I know it's just a matter of time before they find me. I jump to my haunches, trying to decide what to do. *How do you want to die, Samuel? A coward or a warrior?*

I burst from the bush, screaming at the top of my fool lungs, runnin' blindly into the carbon void until I'm stopped in my tracks about a hundred feet out. The bayonet is stuck in something, and when I try to pull it out, it knocks me completely off balance. I don't even realize what it is 'til the weight of the thing pulls me forward and I feel myself falling to the earth.

The entire length of the bayonet had plunged through the chest of a Confederate soldier. It went completely through 'im, and when we crashed to the ground – me on top of 'im – the bayonet imbedded itself fully into the earth to the elbow. Our heads slammed together on the way down and my forehead bashed his nose, breaking it, I think, because blood was gushing alarmingly over the side of his face. The handguard was lodged into his rib cage and there was no way it was comin' out.

We lay there for what felt like minutes staring blankly at one another. Cannons are going off all around us now, landin' real close. The booms are deafening, shakin' the ground, and hundreds of little petals – pink cherry blossoms – are fallin' down on us like snow. One of 'em lands on his eyelid and I think, damn guy, how you gonna get that thing offa there?

Then I look into his eyes, Viola – I mean really look into them. I don't know what I was expectin'. Some sickish monster with three heads and a putrid, oozing Cyclops eye in the middle of each forehead? I don't know. But all I see there beneath me is this terrified kid, fifteen-years-old at most, and it's like I'm starin' straight into a mirror. All I can do is watch as a thick current of blood gurgles in his throat, crests over his lips and seeps into the earth. Hot, steamy gurgling rivers of blood from his nose and throat - and blood from my split lip dripping down, co-mingling with his. This is wrong, just so wrong."

Samuel opens his arms wide on both sides and lets them slap down wearily against his outer thighs. He runs a hand through his hair and sits back in the rocker, nodding, confirming that this is wrong, this is just so wrong.

"So the gunfire surrounds me. Men are running past us – one actually stumbles over us and falls on his face, but gets right back up again. I can't see a goddamn thing, but I know I have to move. I lift myself off the dead boy, yank my rifle from his ribs, and retreat back behind the shed.

That's when the bullet hit me in the leg. I was hunched over a fallen log, shootin' blindly into the field below. Several men from my company joined me. *Shoot, load; shoot, load; shoot, load.* At first it felt like a bee sting. I just ignored it and kept firin' away, but then it started to really throb. I look down, and blood is pulsing from this hole right above my knee and runnin' down my leg like a little river. I remember thinkin', *damn it! I don't have time for this right now!* and I hold my position and keep firin' until we realize our stand is weakening. They're bustin' right through, totally surrounding us, and when it comes time to retreat, I can't. I just couldn't move.

I had no choice but to hunker down behind the log, praying and clutching my leg. Blood was everywhere. My entire pant leg was drippin' with it, and it pumped through my cupped hands and fingers. I was so angry with myself, so mad at havin' put myself in that position. I should've known better. Should've fallen back behind the troops right after I realized I was shot. But your whole sense of time and priority are completely warped by the fear flooding through your veins.

At first I just laid there, waiting for them to find me. Then I crawled into a spot against the shed, under the brambles, hoping they'd pass me by. My breath is heavy – almost to the point of hyperventilatin' – and I close my eyes to calm myself. Breathe deeply (he does this now), one … two … three. When I open my eyes and look beside me, the Confederate boy I killed is sittin' there, touching his face. 'You broke my fuckin' nose,' he says, a look of angst in his eyes. That's when I passed out."

Viola is sitting forward in her rocker, wide-eyed and completely captivated.

"I remember wafting into this delirious stupor every now and again. I was on the back of a wagon. We were trudging through a cornfield at one point, and the jostlin' was driving me nearly insane, 'cause every time we went over a rock or a bump it felt like someone was plunging a dagger into my leg.

Thankfully, I was passed out for most of the journey. When I finally came to, I was lyin' in this thick pool of mud on the ground. I had no idea where I was or how long I was out. Hours only? Maybe days. I woke up slowly, like out of a five-day bender. Tried to open my eyes but they were literally crusted shut. So I just lay there for several minutes, taking in the sounds around me. I knew I'd be able to open them eventually, but wasn't sure I really wanted to.

I knew I was in an open field somewhere, and there were dozens – perhaps hundreds – of moaning men surrounding me. Probably hundreds, because many of them sounded far off. It was a symphony of pain and despair. That's when I realized I was one of them. The pain in my leg was horrific. Someone had put a tourniquet on my upper thigh – I wouldn't be alive otherwise. But the pain. And I was freezing cold.

And the air was unbelievably foul, a stench I pray to never experience again. It was a putrid mix of blood, urine, wool, feces, and decay. So overwhelming I wretched until there was nothin' left in me. It was even worse than smellin' Walter Heslop on fire.

I laid there for days I think, two or three, maybe four. Or maybe it was only hours. My entire concept of time was beyond warped. But I remember thinkin' it had been days, and maybe they thought I was dead.

Eventually they made the rounds to my side of camp. This mangy, toothless prick comes up and kicks me in the thigh, same leg I was shot in. The pain was like nothin' I've ever felt, so it's hard for me to describe it to you now, other than to say it felt like someone had chopped the whole thing off just above the knee with a hacksaw. I tried to scream but couldn't.

Well, this son-of-a-bitch sees I'm alive and drags me halfway across the field by one arm to a filthy wool blanket. There's all these blankets laid side-by-side, dozens and dozens of 'em. Each one has a sick or injured Union soldier lyin' on it. Some of 'em are layin' there spread eagle, in complete dazes like I am. Some are wrapped up in their blankets like mummies, in the fetal position, with only their faces showing. But the guy in the blanket next to me is definitely dead. He's face down, head to one side, starin' at me with milky white eyes, and he's bloated to the point where you think he's just going to start floatin' away at any minute.

So this Confederate bastard walks over to the dead guy and rips a bloody rag from his arm. It's limp, covered with yellow pus and black blood stains. He brings it over to me and crouches over my leg. I'm completely paralyzed, struggling to stay conscious to see just what the hell this guy is gonna do to me. I'm totally powerless to defend myself, completely paralyzed. I mean, I can't even blink. But my mind," Samuel taps his forehead, "my mind is there, and I'm terrified.

I watch him take a grungy tobacco tin from his breast pocket and peel off the lid. Inside is a mound of white maggots, hundreds of them. He takes a big pinch – just like they're really tobacco – and shoves them into the hole in my leg, then he picks up the filthy rag from the dead guy and replaces the sopping tourniquet around my leg. At the time I wanted to kill this man with my bare hands, Viola, but in the long run, I guess I should be thanking him, because he saved my life."

Samuel pauses to drink.

"I drifted in and out over the next couple days. The guards would make their rounds, pokin' you in the ribs to see if you were still alive. Once a day they'd lift my head and force water down my throat, but most times it just came right back up.

During this time I regained some of my movement. Only my head, really, and my arms, but my leg went completely numb. Fever was raging through my entire body, making me hallucinate. Well, I think they were hallucinations, but maybe not; maybe what I was seeing was really happening. I tend to believe the latter, but these I won't share with you, Viola. One thing in my mind was certain, though. I had to get out of this place if I was going to survive. And if I didn't do it soon – very soon – I was probably going to lose my leg to a butcher, then I'd be a dead man for certain.

So over the next several days I fought off the fever as best I could. When they came around with water and cornmeal, I accepted both, and ate 'em slowly to keep 'em down. I studied everything about the place, and the soldiers working it. I became familiar with their patterns, the rounds they did. There was the mess round once a day. Then the maggot bastard did his rounds, once a day also. Then there was the round for body checks. That was done twice a day. First a guy would come around and kick you in the ribs if you weren't obviously alive. If you weren't alive, he'd shout, *'Ripe one!'* at the top of his lungs. Then a second guy would come behind him and proceed to rip everything of value from your body. Pocket watches, coins, belt buckles, food, rings. If your finger was too bloated, he'd just cut it off, and if you had gold in your mouth, then the pliers came out."

Viola winces and covers her eyes with her hands.

"Next was the body wagon. One or two guys sat at the head of the cart, a couple more walking behind. If you were dead, they'd pick you up like a sack of potatoes – one grabbin' your arms, one your legs – send you airborne. When the wagon was full, they'd wheel around to the back of camp, stack bodies in the corner or throw 'em over the fence. At first, they dug big pits to bury 'em in, but then I think they just couldn't keep up, there were just too many. They started puttin' 'em in these big pyramid piles and set them on fire.

So I laid there, takin' this all in. The steaming bakehouse. The makeshift surgical tents. The open cesspool. The camp was built around a spring-fed stream runnin' through the middle of it. You could see its point of origin, where it bubbled pure from the ground, but nothing else about the place was pure at all. Thousands, literally thousands of prisoners used the stream to urinate and defecate in; to bathe in, to drink. I was finally able to prop myself into a sitting position, but I couldn't walk at all, so I dug a hole next to me with my fingernails, and that's what I used as my toilet. A couple times the skies opened up and it poured, then the stream would overflow, and those of us closest to it, our blankets would be saturated.

Late in the afternoon of my fourth or fifth day they brought a new group of injured into camp. The two blankets beside me were empty, and they filled one with a young soldier named Brian Livingston.

Brian was a kid, eighteen, nineteen maybe. Dirty blond hair, big blue eyes. He had a strawberry birthmark on his jawbone, below his right cheek.

Brian was hurt real bad. Had a hole the size of a frying pan in his chest, with a makeshift tourniquet wrapped around his torso. Blood and pieces of tissue – intestine, I guess – were oozing through the rags at several weak points. But he was still alive. I was totally amazed at how coherent he was, and it made me feel ashamed of my inability to keep it together because of a little hole the size of a nickel in my leg. The sun was startin' to go down, and I dreaded the nights, because the mosquitoes out there were as big as goddamned dragonflies.

Brian knew he was dyin'. Over the next several hours he told me his entire story. He was one of twelve children, born to Penelope Pierce and Jacob Barstow of Champlain, Illinois. When he was twelve, he had his first sexual experience with a girl from his church named Patty Johnson, up in the barn loft while his father was out back haying the field. His youngest brother, Michael, was kicked in the head by a horse when he was three. The kid lived through the ordeal but was never quite right afterward, and Brian was constantly nursing black eyes and bloody noses defending him from the bullies in town. He had a girl back home named Cindy Hartford, and they planned to marry when he came home from The War.

Brian kept a picture of Cindy in his jacket pocket. He dug it out to show me. She was plain and unsmilin' in the photograph, but beautiful. Her hair was long and blond, her face round, kind. 'Here, take this, please,' he told me. 'Find her, and let her know I love her.' Then he asked me if I'd hold his hand.

After that, Brian fell into a stupor. He lay there as night fell, mumblin' and strugglin'. Every once in a while he'd shout out *'Mother!'* or *'No!'* or *'Stop!'* But most of it was unintelligible. He went on this way for hours, but never once did he let go of my hand. I fell in and out of a restless sleep myself, but sometime in the middle of the night, Brian's grip on my hand squeezed like a vice.

I struggled to see him - to find his face - but there was no moon that night. Couldn't even make out a vague outline of him. All I could do was lay there and listen, and I kept sayin', *'It's alright, Brian, it's alright.'* I kept holdin' his hand. Then he let out a gurgle and a deep sigh, and his grip on my hand totally slackened and fell away.

The next morning as the sun began to rise, I was able to make him out. When there was enough light to see details, I was thankful his face was turned away from me. I didn't want to see his eyes, murky and vacant like that other dead guy beside me when I first arrived. And that's when it hit me! Two body checks daily. One in the morning, one late afternoon.

I waited until I heard 'em start the body rounds. The spotter went out first, whooping out, *'Ripe one! Ripe one! Ripe one!'* He must've said it two dozen times before the cart started in behind him.

I soiled myself, lyin' there with my eyes open, dead still. An hour went by, then another. A lotta men died that night. The cart filled once, dumped, then once more and dumped. At high noon they still hadn't made it over to us. Brian's body was startin' to bloat and smell real bad.

Finally, the spotter made it over to us. He checked Brian first. Kicked him in the ribs, once, then again. *'Ripe one!'* he shouted. Then he turned to me.

He stared at me for a minute, I mean really stared at me. I was certain he knew. A nervous tick was twitching away just below my left eye, and I knew he was starin' right at it. But then he hauled off and kicked me a good one in the side, here - Samuel grabs his left side - and once more in the same spot, only harder. Then he pauses. *'Ripe one!'* he finally shouts, before moving on.

Next to come is the little scavenger shit. He bends over Brian and starts rummaging through his pockets. I'm lyin' on my side, facing them, so I can see it all. He finds a knife, a tin of tobacco, a pen. No rings to cut off. But then he opens Brian's mouth, and it takes a second to really sink in before I realize. Oh my God, my fillings, I have three gold fillings."

Samuel stops to gauge Viola's disposition. She is sitting in the rocker with both knees pulled up to her chin. She nods fervently and motions for him to continue.

"When he's done with Brian, he moves over to me. He rolls me onto my back, and his stench slaps me in the face. He smells like whiskey and vomit, filthy bed linens. First he checks my fingers. No rings. Next he rummages in my pockets and finds a silver flask, and the picture of Cindy Hartford. He twirls it in his fingers, bites down on it with his back teeth, then he looks at Cindy, and smiles this putrid smile. *'Ugly bitch,'* he says, and throws it into the dirt.

Now come the teeth. The filthy little bastard – excuse the language, Viola, but this really angers me – this filthy little bastard opens my mouth, and he smiles."

"Oh my God," Viola whispers.

"Well, I thought the pain in my leg was bad! I had to dig down, retreat somewhere to the depths of my soul. Out-of-body experience. Somehow I did it, Viola. I don't know how, exactly, but somehow I did it. Divine intervention, perhaps."

Another hour or so went by before the body cart pulled in. At this point pretendin' to be dead wasn't such a difficult task. I could barely take it anymore. It was almost to the point where I didn't give a shit if they found me out or not. Blood was oozing from my mouth, pooling in my throat, almost gagging me, and I remember thinkin', *Do dead men bleed like this? Do dead men bleed?!* I focused all my remaining energy into stifling the reflex to blink, or swallow, or moan.

I was vaguely aware of being picked up and thrown into midair. I landed on top of the pile – on a heap of dead men – and I thought, oh dear Lord, I must be in hell, this must be exactly what hell feels like. Other dead men were thrown on top of me, one after another, after another. I felt myself fading. I think my brain was just on complete overload, and couldn't take anymore. I was being smothered by dead men. I felt myself shutting down. But something in me knew I couldn't do that, 'cause the next thing they were going to do was throw me over the fence and set me on fire. So if I passed out now, I would be burned alive."

"Oh my God," she whispers again.

"The next thing I knew, I was in pitch darkness, in the middle of the night somewhere. The only light I could see was a small campfire with several bodies huddled around it on the other side of the prison. It was far enough away it didn't pose a risk of detection. I climbed my way out from beneath the pile – I was about a third of the way up – slid back down the far side, crawlin' over arms and legs, heads and bloated torsos, and I was free."

Samuel falls silent, and sits down on the stoop not far from where Viola is sitting in the rocker. He runs his hand through his hair and stares out into the pasture.

"That's the first time I've told anyone that story, the first time in thirty-three years."

Viola nods, nearly speechless. "Thank you for sharing

that with me Samuel," is all she can mutter.

They sit together on the porch for another half hour, each of them wrapped in their own thoughts. The sun has almost completely set into the lake. Finally he rises and stretches, picking up his jelly jar. His breath whispers past her, full of sweet whiskey, musky sandalwood. The lantern flickers in the window behind them, and Viola is thankful for the distraction. The oil reserve is almost empty.

"Time for me to head up for the night," he says.

Viola disappears into the house and removes the lantern from the inside sill. "You'll need this to find your way," she says. "Do you have enough blankets?"

He nods and raises his glass to her in a good night gesture before turning away and heading toward the barn.

"Good night, Samuel." She gently closes the screen door behind her.

V

31 May 1898

The barn is now half complete.

Samuel begins to take his meals in the kitchen with Viola. Sometimes they sit at the pine table in front of the hearth, other times they stand at the butcher block, laughing and talking. The transition was an easy one, quite natural and unspoken. Without warning, their relationship had slipped into comfortable intimacy.

Viola finds herself opening to Samuel, slowly revealing bits of her own past, though still holding back. He always listens with attentive patience as she struggles for just the right word, just the right nuance to properly convey her point. And he nods or sighs in all the right places, seeming to understand her sorrow, to identify with it. Viola finds it liberating.

"I was up on the bluff this morning," Samuel says.

They're sitting in the parlour in front of the fireplace, sipping Snowflake. The day had been clear and mild, a refreshing change from the searing heat of the past month. Although the prior week's storms offered a couple mild days of reprieve, the temperature quickly spiked back up into the 90's, where it had remained ever since.

"Ahhh, so that's where you disappeared to."

"Yup. Sure is beautiful up there. You can see forever – the water, the beach, the dunes, rolling hills of green. Must be the most beautiful spot on the entire homestead. I can see why you buried them there."

Viola turns her attention from the mantle, taken aback just a bit.

"Yes, it is a beautiful place," she says finally. "Isn't it?"

She has spoken of her parents to Samuel in a fond and loving way, recounting select "surface" memories from youth. Father always out in the pasture with the cows or working on projects for Mother – a new jelly cupboard for the kitchen, extra shelves in the pantry, a coat rack for the entryway. He had a way with wood and loved to spend time in Andie, "tinker-doodlin' around," as Mother called it.

And she told him that Mother was a lovely woman, tiny and thin. There was a quiet grace about her, and a legendary sense of humor and sharp, dry wit one wouldn't expect from such a little lady. She spent most of her days tending to chores and gardening, ensuring they were all well fed and rested. She was lovely. The pillar of strength that bound them to one another.

"When did you lose them?"

Viola gazes at the picture of her parents on the mantle. They must have only been in their early twenties when it was taken, twenty-some years younger than she is today.

"Mother came down ill in the winter of 1890. Just a spade of influenza we all thought, but she could never quite shake it. It stayed with her through the spring and summer, slowing her down, until all she did was sleep all the time by fall. That winter was a cold one – oh my *Lord*, was it cold. And *snow*. We were all shut in for weeks, huddled in here around the fireplace most days. Mother would sit in the chair you're in right now, covered with blankets. She always had a book lying face down on her lap."

Viola stares into the fire. Funny how she gauged her life along the timeline of the seasons.

"We finally lost her in January."

Viola recounts her final year with Father, his last days in particular, with a detail she didn't believe she was capable of. Making breakfast that morning, finding Father in bed. The painstaking task of constructing his coffin with his own tools. Digging the grave. Dragging his limp body wrapped in muslin and a comforter to the top of the bluff. Plying him with bags of lye to keep the coyotes at bay. And the dread and aloneness that washed over her that day which she has never been able to shake completely. It's true that time is a healing process in itself, but it never quite erases the pang of loss. The scars diminish over the years, but always remain as distant souvenirs.

Samuel notices Viola staring at another photograph on the mantel.

"So, tell me about your husband."

Viola turns to him, then looks back into the fire, smiling faintly.

"His name was Robert. Family owned the Old Bauman Place on the other side of town. Their kin hailed directly from Belfast. Our fathers grew up together and were very dear friends, so we knew each other early on. He was like family. We attended school together, and all the children looked up to him, especially the younger ones. He was very kind and patient, and they gravitated toward him. He had a very special, gentle aura about him. Glowed with it. And he never held back. Gave all of himself to anyone, offering words of encouragement and compassion or playful humor to make even the most difficult situation seem lighter. You always knew everything would be okay, as long as Robert Thompson was around.

I knew from an early age that we would be together. Everyone did. It was just a given. We married in a little sanctuary in Pinnebog when I was sixteen. He was eighteen. Just the two of us and the preacher."

Viola looks into the fire again and plays with the ring still on her left hand as she recounts their wedding ceremony in her head. A ring of red and purple peonies in her hair, with a matching bouquet. A simple dress of purple linen that mother had made. The love shining in Robert's eyes as she walked down the aisle – barefoot - to stand beside him and exchange vows.

"He was my first memory as a child, the most beautiful thing I'd ever seen. I knew he would be mine, even then. We had twelve beautiful years together. I was so incredibly blessed." She smiles, ready to neatly tuck these memories back into bed. "What about you? Do you have any family?"

Samuel lifts the bottle of rum from the table next to his

chair, refilling his jar to the brim.

"Wow, a full-barreled question, I see."

"Oh yeah," he chuckles. "Guess you could say that."

She nods.

"Well, during The War I'd write letters home every week. Long, soulful letters to my mother. Every Sunday, no matter where we bedded down for the night – a soggy field, a naked glen in the dead of Winter – I'd light a lantern and pull out my ink well and whatever paper I could scrounge up over the week, pour my guts out to her. I wouldn't go into any graphic detail or anything, I mean, I was real close to my mother, but no mother should hear such horror from her child. So I'd write mostly about the towns and the beautiful landscapes we passed through. I told her of my dreams for once The War was over, how I'd come home and help her and Pa on the farm, maybe set up a little cabin of my own. Find a wife, give her some grandchildren. Always tried to stay positive. Writing her was my salvation those first two years.

We'd only get mail once a month or so, and by the time her letters reached me they were wrinkled and tattered, three-month-old news. She'd recount her days on the farm with Pa, their trips into the city once a month. She'd write about when I was a child, how much she loved me, how silly and precocious I was even back then, and how the undertones of sadness she read in my letters haunted her.

Well, one month went by without a letter from her, then another. Then a third month and a fourth. I still kept writing every Sunday night, but my words were becoming more strained and desperate, finally pleading. Six months went by, then seven, and by the eighth month I got a whole stack of letters bound together with twine. I was overjoyed!

Somehow the letters from my mother had been lost – I just *knew* it – but as I pulled out my pocketknife to slice the twine, I saw my own handwriting staring back at me. All those Sunday night letters – seven months' worth of Sunday's – all marked 'Return to Sender' in my father's script."

Samuel pauses to clear his throat and take another drink.

"Before you know it, another year goes by. I keep writing those letters, every Sunday night, and they keep coming back for the first six months or so. But then they quit. I was hopeful maybe there was some mix up, some logical explanation as to why Mother didn't write anymore. The ruse was easier to face than the truth. It was the only thing that kept me going, writin' those letters.

After being liberated from Macon, I found my way north again and was holed up in an infirmary for three months in Illinois before my honorable discharge. The first thing I did was hop a train to Minneapolis. Two days later I was making the trek out to Red Wing. I was nineteen, pretty rough around the edges – grubby beard, a limp, at least forty pounds lighter than I am today. They'd fattened me up a bit in the infirmary, but I was still a walkin' skeleton.

It was early May, which can still be relatively cold over in Minnesota. There was snow on the ground, but the robins were returning, and the trees were budding. I finally reached the farm and was floored by this powerful wash of emotion. Of relief, I think, but there was grief there too, and anger for all the time I'd lost. And mostly, I remembered, I was just plumb weary.

Our old farmhouse was just a dot from the main road, a good quarter mile up a dusty, double-rut trail. The closer I came, the more I could tell somethin' had changed, somethin' wasn't right. The grass was waist high, shutters all closed, save for one bangin' in the wind. The barns and corrals and the fields were all empty, not a critter in sight. Looked totally forsaken."

Viola tucks her legs into the chair, holding the jar in one hand as she unconsciously runs a finger in circles around the rim.

"But then the front door opens and Pa steps onto the porch.

He'd aged *unbelievably* – I mean, I almost didn't recognize him. When I'd left for war, he was just starting to grey, but the man before me now had this shock of pure white hair. His clothing was rumpled and stained, and he shuffled onto the porch, hunched and slow-witted. And his *eyes*, Viola. I'd seen that look many times on the field, the look of a lost mind. He had a shotgun cradled in his arms."

A gentle breeze rustles outside, and a branch from the linden tree next to the window scrapes against the pane.

"He stops at the foot of the stairs, legs apart in a show of defiance, lookin' at me with those crazed eyes. *'Who the hell are you?'* he yells at me, and I say, *'Papa, it's me, Samuel!'* He stares at me good and hard for a few seconds, and I thought I saw a flash of recognition there for just a moment, but it was gone. *'Samuel died in The War!'* he yells, *'My boy Samuel's dead! Now get the hell off my property!'* He hoists the barrel to his sights, puts his finger on the trigger. I stood there in disbelief and tried to argue some sense into him, but he was too far gone. Samuel was dead to him, died in The War, and he wasn't gonna have nuthin' to do with this walking corpse standing in front of him claimin' to be his son.

'Git out NOW!' he bellows, firin' a shot that pings off the

dirt in front of me. I can't tell if he meant to miss me on purpose or just got off a bad shot. Here I'd made it through four years of war, and I was about to be shot dead by my father in my own front yard! But I couldn't leave without finding out what happened to Mother. *'Where's Mother?'* I screamed, tears streaming down my face. *'Where's Sally?'* He put the sights in line again, holds me there. *'Sally's DEAD!'* He spits this last like a dirty word and motions with his head over to the front pasture. There's a wood cross there in the middle of the field with tall plumes of wheat grass all around it.

'One final warning!' he tells me then. *'Get the hell off my land!'* I put my hands up and back away down the drive. Turned to look at the house every now and again, and he was still standin' there with the shotgun to his eye. He probably stood there like that even after I was gone."

Viola shakes her head. "I'm so sorry."

He shrugs.

"I snuck back there in the night, when the house was dark, and I was certain he was asleep. I just had to see for myself the name on the marker. And there it was, Sally May Elliott, plain as day."

"So that's the last time you saw him?"

"Yup. Took off for Texas the next day. But all those years later, after Mexico, the Amazon, ten years in Tibet, when I came back to the States again, curiosity got the best of me. I came in on a clipper and eventually made my way back to the old farm again.

A lot had changed in fourteen years. The town was eating its way into the countryside and that fifty-mile walk from Minneapolis was only just seven or eight now. The farm was up and running again. The house was all fixed up and painted a different color, yellow I think, and the barns and pastures were full of cows and goats and chickens. Bank repo, I imagine. But the front pasture was still untouched and overgrown, and there were two markers there now instead of one."

The warmth of the fire is comforting, like a warm blanket on a blustery afternoon. Its flickering sends long shadows dancing across the hearth rug. Samuel's face is glowing, weary. The tree branches scrape against the window. The two of them fall silent.

Viola's eyelids are heavy with whiskey and fatigue, and she closes them. She feels a light and tingly comfort, not sure whether she can peel herself up off the chair. She can feel the warmth of the fireplace against her face, but something else is there with them too, drifting like a swirling mist about the room. The echo of long-ago summers, whispering that their time here is nothing more than a fleeting thought; the flutter of a distant breeze.

Viola opens her eyes again and turns to Samuel. His head is tilted lightly to one side, and he has fallen asleep. She rises slowly and tiptoes to a cupboard on the other side of the room for a blanket, careful not to wake him. She drapes it gingerly over his chest and legs, watching the dancing firelight upon his peaceful face. It is slack now and calm, and she can almost see the boy he once was, the silly and precocious and sad little boy that once haunted Sally May Elliott's dreams.

"Buona notte, Samuel," she whispers, lightly brushing the back of her hand against his warm stubbled cheek before tiptoeing upstairs.

V

1 June 1898

When Viola opens her eyes the next morning, it is raining again.

After dressing and checking herself in the mirror, she makes her way downstairs and tiptoes around the corner to peek into the parlour. The blanket is folded into a neat square on the arm of the chair, but Samuel is gone.

As she gathers pots and pans for breakfast, Samuel enters with a hat full of eggs. The shoulders and upper chest of his denim shirt are wet with rain.

"Mornin'" he says, smiling. He takes them over to the butcher block, setting them down carefully.

"I'll have some coffee started in just a minute," she tells him.

"Oh no here – let me do that." Samuel busies himself grinding beans with mortar and pestle, and their exotic, nutty aroma fills the room. "Doesn't look like I'll get much done again on the barn today," he tells her. "It's not raining hard, just enough to keep me from getting anything accomplished. If it's all right with you, I'd like to take Carl into town after breakfast and stock up on some more paint. You have an account down there at The Mercantile, isn't that right?"

Viola cracks eggs, one by one, on the side of the frying pan. "That's right," she says, "and I don't mind. But how 'bout I go with you?"

The bell on the screen door jangles furiously as Viola enters. Samuel is still out front, securing Carl to one of the hitching posts. The Mercantile is quite busy, and Willy is helping Mrs. Bronson and her young son Timothy select hardware for a front entry gate.

"Oh, this is what you need, right here," he says, dipping his hand into a bucket of nails. "3-inchers. These should do the trick."

Willy looks up as the door slams. That familiar little smirk he seems to reserve just for her creeps onto his lips.

"Good morning, Mrs. Thompson. Back again so soon?"

"Good morning, Mr. Fagan."

The aisles are filled with townsfolk, most of whom she knows. Toddy Hammond is standing in front of a rack of handsaws. He has one in each hand, sawing them back and forth in mid-air at the same time to decide the best fit. Over in Aisle Seven is Crawford Picket and his wife Julienne. She's admiring a cast iron coffee pot, while he's a bit further down the aisle drooling over a new shipment of post hole diggers. Ernest Finney is there too with his second wife Taylor, perusing hoes and rakes and shovels. Now *there* was a scandal Willy had enjoyed. Ernest was in his early fifties and his first wife Roslyn had passed from consumption several years back. Taylor was the daughter of one of the farm hands and couldn't be more than fifteen or sixteen years old. They married only one week after Roslyn died, and she gave birth to the first of their five children just four months later.

Many heads bob between the rows, but Viola really can't make them all out. Rain never fails to bring folks to town, a good opportunity to stock up for when the weather breaks.

The bell above the door jangles again as Samuel enters.

He ducks his head a bit so his hat won't scrape against the jamb, and a spatter of water drips to the floor. He looks up again, finds her immediately, and smiles.

"Can I help you?" Willy titters. *Oh, a stranger. New fodder for the gossip mill.*

"I'm with the lady here," Samuel tells him.

Willy stares at Samuel, then looks over at Viola, and back at Samuel again. He is obviously caught off guard, and just stands there, jaw agape. The entire store is quiet. Everyone has stopped shuffling and comparing and contemplating to focus their attention on the two of them.

"We're just here to pick up some more paint, Mr. Fagan. You can put your eyes back in your head now."

Viola leads Samuel to Aisle Ten and they choose six buckets of red. He takes them outside to load them into Carl's pannier while she stands in line behind three other people. Viola nods at Carla McCleary as she brushes past on her way to the fabric section. Carla makes eye contact for just a second before turning away, ignoring her.

Samuel returns and waits patiently next to her until it's their turn.

Willy has composed himself again, attempting to look puffed up and cocky-confident. Whenever he's behind the counter he does this. Viola believes it somehow makes him feel more important. Official. Authoritative.

"I know, I know, put it on your account."

The store behind her falls completely silent once again, and she can feel all eyes upon them. Viola smiles.

"Yes, please, but I do have one additional purchase." Viola looks past Willy to the endless rows of beer, wine and liquor stacked on shelves against the wall.

Muchener Beer ~ National Brewing Co. "Special Brew"
San Francisco, CA

The Knickerbocker, "Bartholomay's Best Brew"
Wm Wolff & Co, Pacific Coast Agents

Wunder Brewing, "Brewed from Select Malt & Bohemian
Hops; Pure in Every Respect"

Uncle Sam Wine Cellars and Distillery of Napa, CA

Medal Port by Medal Wine Co.
"An Old and Generous Wine for Invalids"

The Independence Cordial, M. Faure
"Fine indeed! My niece let me have another glass!"

Blue Gum Bitters ~ "The Stomach's Friend;
Let its Use be Witness"

Pipifax Magic Bitters, "Restores Youth and Health"
J.W. Goewey and Co.

The Jackass "Celebrated" Kidney & Liver Bitters
by J-S O'Callaghan & Co, Sacramento

Old Judge Kentucky Bourbon ~ Neumark Gruenberg & Co.

Anderson County Sour Mash Whiskey
Louis Taussig & Co.

Old Pioneer Whiskey, A. Fenkhausen & Co.
"Death to Intimidators"

Tom Gin, "Result of a Perfect and Skillful Distillation"
Wrenden Kohlmoos Co.

Old Log Cabin Whiskey, Hall, Lurhs and Co.
"Absolutely Pure; Old and Mellow"

They could run out of most anything in this town – bread,
water, medicines – but they never ran out of booze.

"I'll take a bottle of Old Overholt rye, please, that one
there." She looks over at Samuel, and he nods. Willy's jaw
drops again, and Viola is certain he'll start drooling at any
moment.

"Mr. Fagan?"

Willy grabs the neck of a tall bottle of Old Judge
Kentucky Bourbon.

"No, no, the other one, the one next to it. And make it
two."

Willy fumbles for the Old Overholt. Several bottles
wobble and clang against one another on the shelf. He
recovers quickly, places the bottles on the counter, and slides
them over to her. Samuel leans forward, placing one large
hand around the neck of each. He nods at Willy, and steps
aside to let Viola pass.

"Thank you, Mr. Fagan," she says. "Put *that* on my
account."

Samuel shakes his head as they walk outside to Carl,
chuckling as he carefully fits the bottles into the packs next
to the paint.

"GOD that felt good!" she giggles.

V

5 *June 1898*

Viola and Samuel are sitting on a wool blanket in front of Mother and Father's headstones atop the bluff. Earlier that morning, Viola announced she would be packing them a picnic dinner when they were done painting for the day. She had taken to helping him paint, as it is much more interesting than her mundane chores.

After cleaning up, she busied herself with stuffing a basket full of goodies. Liverwurst and sweet onion sandwiches; porcupine meatballs from last evening's supper; early cucumbers, snap peas and rhubarb from the garden; and a container of mint sun tea.

Star shine begins to twinkle through the dusky sky just as they're finishing the feast, quite satisfied and relaxed.

Samuel is laying casually on his side, head propped up with one arm. His boots are off and he's wiggling his toes in the grass. "That was perfect, Viola. Thank you so much. What a nice way to end the day."

"I agree," she says, smiling shyly.

She lays down on her back, just a jar of sun tea between them. He is staring down the beach toward the Bay Port Hotel, and she is looking straight up into the sky, watching twinkling shimmers of faint light becoming brighter as the sky darkens. She loves how they can be together and not find it necessary to speak all the time. It's also that way during the day as they're painting side-by-side. Nothing more exhausting than having to fill up empty space with chatter. They're compatible that way.

Samuel moves to lay on his back as well.

"I remember," he starts, when I was in Macon, the only time I found any beauty in that hellish place was at night. I would block out the moaning and look up in the sky." He raises his arm and points. "Right there – you can see Sagittarius just starting to come out. And over there – Lyra, Hercules." Viola strains to see the constellations as they begin to pop.

"Father used to bring me up here to look at the stars," she says. "I wonder if we could have been stargazing at the same time? You from Georgia, me from here in my nightgown."

They turn their heads and smile at one another.

"Could be," he says, "but I like this much better."

"Me too."

V

17 June 1898

Day number thirty-three since Samuel's arrival has drawn to a close.

The screen door bangs shut as Viola walks onto the porch, one sweaty jar of sun tea in each hand. She offers one to Samuel.

"Thank you," he says, closing his eyes and drinking heartily.

As Viola watches him, she feels a blush rise to her cheeks, once again contemplating those strong, brown hands, toughened by years of use and experience - though at the same time, graceful, almost feminine. He opens his eyes and she turns away, praying the flush is not as telling as it feels. She clears her throat and sits down on the rocker nearest the stoop where he is resting and looks to the pasture.

The sun is just beginning to dip, nearing that wonderful shade of blaze so right and familiar to a warm June eve. Samuel is looking toward the pasture as well, with a shy hint of smile across his lips - one he seems to possess most of the time, as one with his gentle demeanor often does. Or maybe it doesn't exist in his pale pink lips and the curve of graying mustache so much as in the warmth of his eyes, a color of blue so rich and deep it brings forth an image in Viola of sparkling blue diamonds in a virgin mine of deep perfection, whose icy brilliance fade only just a slight in the harsh light of midday.

"I remember an evening just like this one," he says, keeping his gaze on the pasture. "It was down in Louisiana, just outside New Orleans, down in the Bayou. This was only a year, two maybe after The War, and I was visiting with another young man from the 2nd Minnesota Infantry Regiment – David was his name, but we called him T-Bone, 'cause he was skinny as a scarecrow. T-Bone McWilliams. T-Bone and me were the only ones that survived from Company A. Sixty-eight men, and just the two of us made it. Imagine that." Viola watches the smile flicker for just a moment, and he turns to meet her eyes before looking away again.

"It was July or August – hot as hell in those parts that time of year. T-Bone went back to live with his folks after The War and was having a hard time keeping himself together. Papa McWilliams ran a little moonshine business for himself down there, and David was finding it difficult to stay outta the hooch." Samuel drains his glass, and wipes droplets of tea from his mustache with the back of his hand.

"Would you like another?" she offers.

"No thank you."

A light breeze flutters through the chimes.

"Well, T-Bone had this sister named Rose – Gypsy Rose, I called her. Skin as dark and smooth as liquid sunlight, and hazel eyes that bore through the core of your soul.

Rose was seventeen, but with a wisdom bred deep of a woman twice her age. She was quiet and somewhat reflective, takin' it all in before offering verbal observation about anything. Never went to proper schoolin' a lick in her life, but that girl had knowledge I still to this day don't fully understand.

On my third night there, after T-Bone and Papa McWilliams had their fill of drink and conversation for the day, Rose took me by the hand and led me to a dock on the edge of the swamp. The sun was at the point it is right now," he lifts his hand toward the sky, "just on the verge of settin', but the color – good Lord – talk of fire and heat – heat in thick waves, moisture so heavy you could taste it, or cut it." He let his hand fall back to his lap. "Have you ever been to the Bayou, Viola?"

She shakes her head. "No."

Samuel closes his eyes and breathes deeply.

"Take a deep breath," he tells her, and she does, filling her lungs and letting the air back out again, slowly.

"Okay, it's late August, and the air is so humid it damn near smothers you. Hard to breathe or move; clothing hangs on you like wet rags, and the scent – can you smell it? Close your eyes."

Viola closes her eyes.

"It's a combination of raw earth and rot – but not

unpleasant, mind you. More sublime, more primitive, but sweet-like, of dying jasmine and moss and still murky waters."

Viola nods.

"What do you see? No, no – keep your eyes closed. Tell me what you see."

Viola smiles.

"The pond I played in as a child, down over the other side of the bluff. It's late in summer; cicadas call thick and strong. A thin film covers the brown water, and little spider bugs are skimming across the top. Anthonie and I used to catch tadpoles and put them in Mother's bell jars, and we'd bring them home to place in a bucket on the porch and feed them flies and pieces of grass and dandelion, hoping they'd grow into frogs. We'd come home covered in muck to our knees and Mother would scold us and make us keep our boots on the back stoop to dry for days."

She laughs, remembering Anthonie's little face, rosy with sunburn; tiny hands darting beneath the surface of the pond to catch slimy tadpoles.

"And what does it smell like?"

Viola takes in another breath and holds it for a moment, smelling the pond, the overgrown sweet grass and blackberry vines.

"Sweet – yes! Sweet berries and green all around; grass and dirt and that earthy scent of decay rising from the pond. Stagnant, almost, but with an underlying sweetness. That scent rises above it all somehow, mingles with it; transforms it into something right and pure."

"Now, tell me how it feels, Viola."

Viola pauses and is aware of the warm sun on her face and arms. But is it the sun above them now, or the warmth of childhood past? Of timeless youth, and living in the moment?

"Well, it's – it's warm, but my legs are cool, they – "

"No, no, not how you feel physically. What are you thinkin'? What are the emotions running through the mind of that child in the murky pond?"

Viola pauses again, taken aback. *Emotions? My God, how do I feel? When was the last time another human being was concerned with my emotions? When was the last time I felt anything other than numb?*   She swallows hard, and tears well in her eyes.

"I –"

"How do you feel, Viola?"

Viola opens her eyes, and Samuel is staring at her. A lone tear rolls down her cheek, and he reaches forward to brush it away. His touch is even more gentle than she had imagined.

"I feel pure and whole, and … carefree. I feel joyful and innocent, and – and *alive*."

He nods.

"Yes, alive," she repeats.

V

18 June 1898

Viola calls for Samuel in earnest. He runs from the garden where he was harvesting asparagus and rushes into the barn to join her.

"Mucca is straining - I think the calf is stuck."

Samuel sits on his haunches to observe. "How long has

she been this way?"

"I'm not sure. She was fine when I checked on her earlier this afternoon. Seemed a bit uncomfortable, but not in labor - at least not like this.

Mucca is laying on her side, her labored breathing causing her huge frame to rise and fall rapidly. Her baby's feet are protruding from the birth canal and her eyes are large and searching. She hears Viola's voice and lifts her head with a pathetic 'mooooooo.'

"Oh girl, I'm here," she says, kneeling next to the distressed heifer, gently stroking her.

Samuel comes around to the backside of Mucca to survey her situation more closely. He bends down to touch the tiny hooves protruding from the mother before going to the far side of the barn near Father's wagon to retrieve a length of rope to act as a sinch.

"Okay," he starts, "we need to try and get Mucca to her feet – then I'm gonna sinch the calf's legs and give her an assist."

Viola nods. She rises and prods Mucca into a standing position. The heifer is wobbly on her feet, legs splayed and stumbling forward.

"We need to do this quick," he tells her.

Viola comes round to the front of the heifer, scratching her ears and talking gently.

"It's okay girl, va bene, dolcessa. We're gonna help you out here."

Samuel sinches the rope around the calf's hooves and begins to pull, gently at first. Mucca brays loudly and begins to pull against Samuel in an effort to release the calf. They rock back and forth for several minutes in a trance dance before the baby suddenly spills out of Mucca into a puddle on the bedding hay.

"It's a bull!" he exclaims. Mucca immediately turns around and goes to her baby, beginning to clean him off with her tongue.

"Successo!" Viola proclaims, throwing her arms around Samuel. "Thank you! Thank you!" She pulls away from him, surprised by her own reaction. He is surprised also, as he is three shades of red. She settles into a corner of the stall to watch Mucca and her new son.

"Happy to help," he tells her. "I'm gonna wash up and then I'll start a fire, if that's okay."

"That would be great - we can eat outside tonight. It's beautiful out."

After dinner, Samuel goes up to the barn to retrieve his violin while Viola carries the dishes inside. They meet back at the humble fire and she settles into her rocker for the evening with two jelly jars full of Old Overholt.

"Here you go," she says, handing one to him. He takes a big swig and wipes his mouth with the back of his hand.

Samuel moves with quiet grace as he pulls a handkerchief from his back pocket and kneels down next to Viola. His shoulder is close enough to almost brush against her knee, and a twinge of current radiates through her. His breath whispers past, full of sweet whiskey - and the scent of him — of fresh air and hot evening moisture - makes her a tad headier than she already is from the liquor they're drinking in the wane of twilight.

Samuel squats on his haunches in front of the battered

pine case and gingerly unhooks the hinges, a ritual performed hundreds – perhaps thousands – of times past. Viola watches him remove the instrument from its casing with great care, caressing the fine grain as though the thigh of a lover.

The violin was handmade from pine and mahogany. The strings are held taught by ivory tipped pegs beneath a carefully carved lion head scroll. The edges of the lower boat are a tad worn in the place where Samuel tucks the instrument under his chin, and there is a small dent near the bridge which has darkened and smoothed out over the years. As Samuel turns it over, she can see what looks like names or places carved on the back.

Samuel rises and cradles the instrument across his chest. He pats the stool, motioning her from the porch.

"Come here m'lady. You're going to get a free concert tonight."

Viola throws her head back and laughs as she moves toward the stool.

"A free concert!"

When she is settled, he motions in a circle.

"Turn around, please."

"What?"

Samuel lowers his eyes. Cheeks blushing, he regards his boots.

"You can't watch me play. It – I – you must turn away."

Viola nods and turns round upon the stool. The fire's warmth radiates against her backside. She listens to the faint scrapings of strings readied with resin; slight boot shuffle as Samuel positions himself in stance and clears his throat. Curiosity overcomes her, and she slowly turns to peek over her shoulder.

Samuel has turned away from her as well, shoulder blades swelling through denim as firelight dances upon silver curls at the base of his neck. She watches his elbows strike fiddler's pose, and as he turns his face toward her, just slightly, she admires his lightly stubbled cheekbones, clearly defined, as he lifts the instrument to the crest of his chin and closes his eyes.

Viola quietly turns to watch. Her breath catches in her throat as fervent strains of melancholy burst upon the night, racing and intertwining with sparks spiraling into the black sky. It is the same melody she heard him play on the beach, and then again in the early morning hours from the hayloft. A sweet, mournful note, drawn long and held high. It is both eerie and entrancing, commanding full attention – the beckoning call of a lone, hypnotic siren. Viola's heart quickens as the melody creeps into her chest with an obscure breadth and depth of sorrow, of soulful despair. Samuel's eyes remain closed, lips pressed in conviction, and he sways in one fluid stroke with the music until she can't quite discern where the instrument ends and he begins.

Moonlight through the pines
Starshine on the lake
Will you and I be together once more, dear one
Or shall we leave this love behind?

The music ends, yet Samuel's eyes remain closed as he slowly lets the instrument drop against his thigh. *He's shaking*, she notices, as he bows his head momentarily before stretching to full posture, raising muscular arms wide open to the night, and sighing with great satisfaction. As he turns, Viola quickly spins around again, clasping her hands in her lap until the knuckles turn white. She feels as though she may burst into tears.

He sits down on a stool in front of the fire, exhausted. "How was that?" he says, beginning to play again, a lighthearted, spontaneous refrain of unknown origin.

Viola turns slowly, chest heaving. A gentle smile spreads across Samuel's face, the sparkle in his eyes having surrendered to a glazed serenity, a quiet calm. His craft transforms him. The look on his face is familiar. He is drained, though deeply satisfied, as though gazing into the eyes of a lover.

"Enchanting," she whispers.

Viola rises and slowly walks to Samuel, around to the back side of him. She reaches out, tentatively, and places a trembling hand upon his shoulder. He pauses play for a moment and turns his face just slightly in her direction before resuming.

Viola runs her fingers slowly down his shoulder, tracing tight muscles as he pours himself into his instrument once again. She slides her hand lower between his shoulder blades, ever so gently, with the slightest caress. Samuel continues his pace as her fingers slide upward to toy with the gleaming silver curls at his neckline. He plunges into one last fervent burst of melody before stopping abruptly and lowering the violin to his knee. She is massaging his right shoulder now, thrilled by the heat emanating through his denim shirt.

"I saw you," he says, "that night on the bluff, watching me."

Viola moves in front of him, and gently brushes his stubbled cheek with the back of her hand. He nuzzles into her, sighing deeply.

"You smelled of roses."

Viola extends her hand, and Samuel stares into her gaze. His warm hand completely engulfs her slender fingers as he rises.

"You are so beautiful," she whispers.

Six

Lovers

Viola is floating just below the ceiling, looking down upon herself, at the two of them. Their humid bodies reflect shine in flickering lantern light, entwined upon rumpled white bed linen.

Samuel lay beside her with one knee resting over her thigh. She welcomes his open mouth upon hers, and slowly runs her tongue across his trembling lips before pulling away to brush against his shoulder, to taste him. He is salty sweet and something more - something wild and earthy like the exotic, coarse scent of myrrh, of longing. His hands slide across her body.

He lay beside me
breath upon my breast
hands upon me

and I wonder, ponder so
what shall befall me
for experiencing such rapture?

Viola is vaguely aware of being engulfed by this ritual of expression and domination, one that has whispered undertones of rage – possession – abandonment – since the beginning of time. The breadth of Samuel is overwhelming, as if they are melding into one implicit creature.

And once betwixt the witching hour
to lay with my love
the recollection of his touch so sublime
I tremble.

The heady pulse of adrenaline
of instinct
muscular grace of tendon and bone

Whispers brush the spine
lips across the brow
and how I do mourn!

Of bone to soul
blood to flesh
pulsing to that which is eternal.

His gasp, my longing.
His pain, my tears.
His loss, my rage.

Our entire lives we have been moving toward one another,
toward this very moment.

"My sweet Viola," he whispers into her hair, "you've finally come to me."

19 June 1898

Viola wakes the next morning to the rousing tune of Yankee Doodle Dandy coming from the yard. It is not quite sunup and the bed next to her is empty. She props herself on one elbow and rubs the haze of slumber from her eyes.

She is naked, wrapped in cool rumpled sheets, and glimpses of last evening send her stomach into a flutter of sweet butterflies.

"There was Captain Washington
Upon a slapping stallion
A-giving orders to his men
I guess there was a million!"

Smiling, Viola wraps the sheet around her body and shuffles to the window.

Samuel is standing in the middle of the yard, giving a free concert to Carl and Mucca, who are staring at him in what appears to be dumfounded wonder. Little chicken heads peer cautiously from the coop as Samuel ceases his singing and delves into a passionate whirl of chord. He pauses once more, violin raised to the sky in one hand, bow in the other, and with carefree abandon belts out more lyrics to the rising sun at the top of his lungs in his gritty baritone.

"Yankee Doodle, keep it up
Yankee Doodle dandy
Mind the music and the step
And with the girls be handy!"

Aside from his boots and hat, he is completely naked.

Samuel's exhibitionism lasts another ten minutes, and when he turns toward the house, Viola rushes back to bed to pretend she is sleeping. He crawls beneath the sheet and reaches for her…

Two hours later, gentle sunlight filters into the bedroom, waking Viola. She opens her eyes and stares at the lacey patterns cast upon the far wall. Samuel's back is turned away, and she lays there for several minutes, watching the rhythmic rise and fall of his breath. The comforter lay across his legs, though his muscular back and the fine swell of one hip are exposed. *So beautiful.*

A long, half-moon scar curves in a perfect arc from Samuel's lung, on the left side, down toward his kidney. She touches it, traces its length on warm, smooth skin. As her fingers travel slowly along the deep indentation, she moves closer and bends down to gently brush her lips along its length from beginning to end. Samuel stirs but does not turn.

Viola presses her naked breasts against his back. She wraps her arm around his body and plays with curly chest hair. Samuel moves to accommodate her, hugging her against him.

"Good morning," he says, clearing his throat.

"Good morning."

V

20 June 1898

"So, whad'ya wanna be when you grow up?"

Viola giggles and splashes at Samuel with her foot. He

grabs it with one of his large hands, gently kneading her toes. They are soaking together in the barn after a full day of painting and gardening, passing a bottle of Old Overholt and a cigar between them. Samuel is wearing his slouch hat, and the water is cool, refreshing.

"Let's see, what do I want to be ..." Viola takes the plump cigar from his lips and places it between her own. A lazy swirl of smoke drifts to the rafters, and she tilts her head back to watch it melt into the evening sun.

"Well, when I was young – twelve, thirteen - I always fancied I'd set off on the ferry someday, head on down to Detroit or Chicago. Maybe hook up with a theatre troop or the circus. Travel the country! End up down south somewhere, southwest maybe."

Samuel's laughter is full and hearty. "A gypsy!" he hollers, his eyes sparkling. He takes a swig from the bottle before letting it dangle in his hand over the side of the basin. "Woman after my own heart!" He trades her the bottle for the cigar, which he promptly cocks in the corner of his mouth, and removes his hat to place it on top of her head.

"A gypsy, yes," she says, "just like you."

Viola moves one foot beneath the water to rest between Samuel's legs. He sinks lower until his chin touches the water, and she can feel him responding. He is smiling.

Viola crouches to her knees and rises to stand fully naked in the basin before him. Water courses down her slim body, and she likes the admiration she sees in him, his wanting her. The hat remains atop her head as she steps carefully out of the basin, and with a shy little smile, walks toward the staircase in the far corner of the barn that leads to the hayloft.

Bales fill two-thirds of the loft, stacked ceiling high in

most places. Over in the far corner, next to an open window, is Father's old lantern, resting on an empty whiskey barrel. Several blankets lie on the floor next to it, all neatly folded and stacked, one on top of the other, and Viola can still see the indentation of Samuel's body in the bed of hay. The boards creak behind her.

Samuel is staring at her, staring *into* her. His eyes reflect the golden sunlight blazing through the window and radiate with his longing. But there is something else there too, something deep and wondrous that draws her into them, propels her from the empty abyss of her past.

V

21 June 1898

The next morning Viola's eyes flutter open and she is surrounded by the scent of roses and sweet peas. She rubs her eyes and sits upright, delighted to find dozens of flowers surrounding her in a full body halo.

The indentation of Samuel's body in the hay is all that remains of him this morning. She rises and walks to the open window to find him putting out new hay for Mucca and her son.

"Hey there handsome!" she yells from the rafters.

He sees her and waves.

Seven

Bittersweet

28 June 1898

The barn is complete.

Viola has enjoyed watching the transformation. Before Samuel's arrival, she was shabby, yet sturdy, faded, but lovely. The first strokes of brilliant red felt like blood on an open wound, but with the passing of each day became more of an awakening, a rebirth, like a woman of middle-age dolling herself up to go into town.

She looks to the sky, bright blue and clear as far as the eye can see. Only a couple lazy white clouds float about, here and there. She feels a little twinge of disappointment, finds herself wishing for rain. She has enjoyed the comfort of the daily routine they have fallen into. The male / female roles that come so instinctually are kind and familiar, and Samuel had transitioned into her bedroom with the same quiet ease as he had her kitchen.

The future has gone unspoken between them, which is befitting of the way they relate to one another. Their sharing is a rebirth in itself, a soothing healing process for them both, and the physical dimension of their relationship is a liberation rather than compulsion, or obligation.

Viola wonders, watching him now as he stretches atop the ladder carefully surveying the splintered wood for any spots that need one final coat, what it would feel like to have him there with her indefinitely.

V

5 July 1898

Viola opens the armoire. Canvas work pants, stained at the knees. Tattered plain work blouses. Even the few skirts she has are rumpled old linen, stained, worn in the garden on hot days for relief. There is sand in the bottom of the armoire, falling from rolled up pant cuffs. *Pants are so unladylike they say, unorthodox.* But nothing about Viola Thompson is conventional. A woman who wears pants; openly purchases bottles of whiskey; smokes cigars. *Damn them all.*

In the back of the armoire, she finds it. A lovely white cotton and lace dress with a built in corset and ruffles to emphasize the décolletage. She bought it one day at market ten years ago from Lily Thorogood. She had never worn it, though she fancied she might someday.

Viola pulls the dress from the hanger and steps out of her clothing before slipping it over her head and looking into the full body mirror. She fusses with her hair, releases the clip and lets it cascade about her shoulders. A few dabs of rouge to the cheeks, rose water down the crest of her bosom, pink lip stain. She has no shoes that would sufficiently match such a lovely dress so she decides to go barefoot. She reaches for the heart locket that Father had given her in her teen years and opens it. Inside is a tiny photograph of Robert. She closes the clasp and decides against wearing it, and before heading back downstairs, she removes her wedding ring and tucks them both into a drawer in her nightstand. She looks out the window and sees the warm flickering of light in the barn as dusk slips away.

The barn is glowing. Samuel stands in the wane evening light spilling through the back door, his shadow elongated across the dirt floor. Viola notices that his clothing is fresh. He had scrubbed them out and let them dry in the sun all day.

Candles are everywhere. All over the floor, on the work benches, along the stalls. They are vanilla-colored beeswax candles she made over the last couple of winters and stored in the cellar. It must have taken him an hour to place and light them all. Viola stands there for a few moments taking in the beauty. He senses her presence and turns.

"Wow," is all he says, moving toward her. He extends his hand, engulfing hers. He is warm.

Samuel leads her to a stool in the middle of the floor, surrounded by flickering light and the scent of fresh paint. *It feels sacred in here,* she thinks, *as though I need to whisper.* As she sits on the stool, he brushes his lips against the back of her neck.

"A free concert?" she asks, smiling.

Samuel retrieves his violin from the case on one of the work benches and positions himself in front of her. This time he stands before her and doesn't ask her to turn.

"You look stunning," he says, smiling back at her. Viola swallows, and her heart actually flutters, to her surprise. A sheen of sweat has begun to dampen her neck and chest.

Samuel closes his eyes and delves into a whorl of string and movement, twisting and swaying, removing his chin from the rest and shaking his head, lost in the chorus. She recognizes the melody that has haunted her late nights, the one that drifts to her at unexpected times throughout the day, melancholic, tragic, filled with such beauty that tears well in her whenever he plays. This time is no exception. They spill over the brims of her lower lids and slowly slide down her cheeks, dripping into her bodice. *How wonderful, tears of joy, rather than despair.*

When the tune has played through he opens his eyes and she smiles. He places the violin back in its case and comes to her again, taking her hand as she rises to greet him. He wipes the tears away and brings her into an embrace, guiding her into a gentle sway as he hums. His hands and brow are damp, and she welcomes his moisture as he brushes his cheek against her forehead, lets his hand drift down the curvature of her spine.

"Your laughter," he whispers, *"the magic of swaying as one. I'll remember you long after, my love; the evening slips into dawn."*

He lifts a hand to cup her face and brings his lips to hers.

"Moonlight through the pines, starshine on the lake. Will you and I be together once more, dear one? Or shall we leave this love behind?"

8 July 1898

"Walk with me."

Viola peers up from Mother's tattered first volume of "A Collection of Poems by Several Hands" and places it face down in her lap. They had enjoyed an early supper and were resting in the parlour, sipping on a lovely concoction of chamomile and lavender tea, an infusion Mother used to make for Father on Sunday evenings.

"A walk?" she inquires. Samuel is standing next to the window, mug in hand, watching the sky. It is late afternoon. The clouds have begun to move in, and the scraping of linden branches against the pane foretell possible showers. He turns to her and smiles.

"Sure," she says. She places her book on the coffee table and then fetches a shawl and changes out of her house slippers.

The screen door slams behind them as they walk onto the porch and are greeted by the mild scent of sweet alfalfa on the breeze. Viola closes her eyes and smiles.

They stroll along the trail in comfortable silence, ambling at a casual pace. Viola extends her hand and lets her fingers brush against Queen Anne's Lace growing along the edge, gently wiggling her fingers to displace tiny black seeds that cling to her skin. She wonders in passing where they may be headed, but decides it isn't quite important enough to inquire.

She is several paces behind when they reach the main road. Samuel turns left and pauses to wait for her.

The wind has kicked up a notch, rustling through oak and maple to extract the occasional leaf and send it into a fervent skyward spiral, a frantic dance of happenstance. Whisked into another burst, and another, until eventually finding its way to the road amidst skittering summersaults before disappearing into the brush.

Viola's mind is calm, unusually void of murmur. She looks up at Samuel's expressionless face as he stares straight ahead. This stroll does not feel as though without purpose, but again, Viola finds it unimportant to question. He senses her gaze, and winks.

Samuel has stopped in the middle of the road and is staring north. His head is tilted slightly skyward, the silver curls at the base of his neck bouncing in the wind. He is fixated on something.

Viola looks up.

BAY PORT CEMETARY

When Viola's presence of mind returns, she takes a step back.

"What?"

Samuel has turned and is watching her.

Viola starts to tremble. She tries to find Samuel's face – to read his intention - but he has become a distant blur of shadow against a backdrop of swaying green pine.

Come visit us, Viola.

Samuel stirs and is sucked back into focus with the force of a slap - although everything around her has drawn completely silent. The trees stir franticly, though there is no howling wind song; leaves scatter about her feet, though their rustlings are absent. A bird flies overhead, struggling in desperation against the gale, but its protests, if any, are non-existent.

Samuel has extended his arm. His face is calm, slack of emotion, though his eyes are warm and beseeching.

"It's alright Viola," he says, as though whispered through the distance of a great tunnel.

Viola ...

She steps forward and extends a shaking hand. Samuel squeezes it tightly as she closes her eyes. Silent wind blowing in lofty gusts, tangling her hair about her face and eyes, whipping her shoulders - hiding her. Shadows are seeping deep into the cemetery in the disappearing late day sun.

Viola lets herself be drawn to the wrought iron gates and waits patiently while Samuel pushes with all his weight to allow them entry. The mighty *creak!* that accompanies such effort is missing.

Samuel gently takes her hand again and leads her inside.

Viola?

She looks up at Samuel, waiting patiently beside her.

Viola darling, I'm over here...

Why is he just standing there, staring at me? she wonders, then realizes he is waiting for her to show him the way.

Viola begins to walk the narrow trail that leads to the far end of the cemetery. She brushes away swaying limbs and whipping mosses, and flinches as a pinecone pelts her shoulder, another atop her head.

And then she sees it.

V

Hello Viola. My Sweet Viola...

She stands above a modest grey marker of limestone. It is mossy around the edges a bit more than anticipated – much more, certainly, than Mother's and Father's. But what did she expect, really? They have only been gone for five and seven years, and this is the first time in twelve years she has stood upon her husband's grave.

Robert J. & RJ Wallace
Together as One

Viola brushes her fingers against the cold inscription.

"Hello, my dear Robert."

She kneels before the headstone, and brushes away fallen limbs and leaves. Scraggly clumps of grass have grown about the base, and she pulls them out and casts them away. Dirt embeds itself beneath her nails. The wind has returned, though only a distant whisper.

Silent tears stream down Viola's cheeks.

"I've missed you so."

Samuel takes a tentative step forward and bends down next to her.

"Oh," she whimpers. Her eyes close, breath calm.

Samuel touches her shoulder, and she flinches.

"Oh," she says aloud, reaching for him.

Samuel brushes the blowing hair from Viola's face and attempts to offer shelter while guiding her to a standing position. She pulls away and opens her eyes, staring directly into him. Her lashes are dewy, eyes wide and vacant. She brushes a hand gently against his cheek in hollow recognition.

Lightning flashes about them in the churning sky, followed ten seconds later by a brazen clap of thunder. The storm is almost upon them. Samuel surveys their surroundings and his eyes land on a blockhouse in the far reaches of the cemetery, near the bone well. He hugs her close and ushers them in that direction.

The blockhouse was here long before the cemetery, a structure used, similar to those out West, to watch for intruders who meant the settlers harm. The last of the Native Americans in the area had departed almost 40 years ago, so the threat is long gone, if ever at all.

Viola crumbles into a corner of the blockhouse and covers her face with her hands. A weariness has descended upon her greater than that of a fever, and she finds it difficult to move.

Samuel sits down next to her and takes her into his arms. She raises her face to him and brushes her lips against his neck. He holds her closer and buries his face in her hair, breathing deeply as she places her hand on his belt buckle.

Another flash of lightning, followed by a crack of thunder only five paces away this time, and the rain begins as huge spatters upon the blockhouse roof. Wind blasts through the small windows where rifles once rested, watching for danger. The storm is upon them.

Viola's lips find Samuel's as he reaches down to caress the top of her bodice, damp with tears. She places her hand atop his, encouraging him to cup her breast as he guides her down to the blockhouse floor. She turns over to her stomach and positions herself. His initial thrusts scrape her cheek against the splintered flooring, embedding two large slivers into her cheek and drawing blood. She cries aloud, and all at once is overcome by visions of fire - chemical fog - burning flesh and screaming - before blacking out.

Her eyes flutter open. The sun has found its way through one of the blockhouse windows and is shining on her face. The storm has passed and Robin song surrounds her. It is morning.

Viola sits upright and winces at the immense throbbing in her left cheek. She reaches up to touch it and feels the end of a large sliver poking through the skin. She grasps it between the nails of her index finger and thumb and yanks, crying out. Her fingers draw away, bloodied. It is the size of a toothpick. There is another, but it will have to wait until she has access to a mirror back home.

Viola stumbles to her feet and exits the blockhouse. She steps over large branches and damp leaves as she makes her way from the cemetery to the main road.

Eight

Descent

9 July 1898

The painting she had started yesterday afternoon – the one with the big brown gash across the canvas – was blown off the porch and lay face down in the mud. The turpentine jar full of brushes is also on the ground, bleeding muted shades of blue, red and black into the muck.

The house is much as she left it. A bucket of potatoes on the chopping block, next to a dark pool of dried blood where she cut herself a while back. An empty jelly jar in the sink.

She walks upstairs to find the bed made, her nightgown laid across the foot of it as she did every morning after making up the sheets and blankets. She walks outside again to find Mucca and Carl wailing their protest at empty hay boxes. Henry and the girls are milling about, and a couple of eggs lay next to the chicken coop, baking in the early morning sun.

Viola goes back into the house and retrieves a hand mirror and tweezers from her dressing table. She takes them downstairs to the kitchen, where the light is best this time of day, and props it up against the potato bucket.

The left side of her face is swollen from her lips to slightly below the lower eyelid. A red hole with crusted blood lay under her cheekbone, the spot where she extracted the first splinter. The second, just slightly above it - and even larger than the first - is still jammed into her cheek.

Viola lifts the tweezers with a trembling hand and tries three times to grab the tip of the splinter to no avail. Each time she touches the area, a stab of pain courses through her face, throbbing in time with her heartbeat.

"Shit," she mutters. On the sixth try, the sliver slips out. She watches in the mirror as a trickle of blood slips down her cheek, pausing just slightly on the crest of her jawbone before dripping to the surface of the block, in the same spot as the old bloodstain.

"Sorry Viola," she says. "That one's not comin' out."

V

16 July 1898

That night Viola is awakened by Samuel's screams.

She fumbles to place herself, straining in the moonlight to find him. He is moaning and thrashing beside her, and Viola's hands tremble as they move to his chest to shake him. "Samuel wake up!"

"Nooooooo!" he wails. He lurches to a sitting position and swats at her, his eyes glazed and wild. He strains away from her and almost falls off the bed before recognizing her.

"Oh God ... Viola."

Samuel reaches out and she takes his clammy body into her arms. He buries his face in her neck as she rubs his back and shoulders, and her hands become damp with his moisture. After several minutes his breath calms. He pulls away to wipe his face, to rid himself of the remnants of his night terrors, and he flops wearily on his pillow to stare at her in the light of the full moon.

"I was seventeen again," he says, "back in battle. Crouching waist deep in filthy muck and reeds in some foul backwater. I was overcome by this horrible sense of foreboding, like something was watching me. Suddenly this black panther pounces through the fog. It heads straight for me - bears down and holds me under water as it rips into me."

Viola reaches out, but he brushes her away.

"As it consumes my flesh, I become the panther. I'm empowered by it. I can feel it move – can hear its thoughts on an abstract, savage level. We see a rat and stalk it, and just as we're ready to pounce we break into this bright wash of sunlight. We're not in the water anymore. We're on that battlefield just outside Corinth, and it's not a rat between my paws, but that boy I stabbed with my bayonet."

Samuel turns away to stare at the moon.

"I bear down and start tearing into his flesh, shredding it away with my teeth and claws. I find his heart; rip it from his body. It hangs from my jowls, dripping with his blood, but when I look down into his face, Viola, it isn't the boy anymore. It's you."

The morning he left, she'd been sitting on the porch, waiting while he gathered his few meager belongings into his knapsack. He had taken them from the barn the morning

after they'd first made love, had placed them on the chair next to the window in her bedroom. She heard the familiar creek of the stairs as he walked down them, and her body stiffened.

Samuel stepped onto the porch, careful not to let the screen door slam. He stood there, tall and lean, dark circles under his eyes, wrinkles like cracks in fine china framing them. There was a tinge of melancholy there, but something else too, something she'd grown quite fond of this past month-and-a-half. They sparkled with kindness and laughter, and knowing him such a short time as this seemed absolutely absurd to her. Samuel could read her thoughts and emotions as though his own, as though they'd been connected for decades. And somehow, they had been. She didn't know how it could be possible, but it was true.

Viola was numb, on the verge of tears. She could feel them coming on – could even see in her mind's eye the blubbering fool she'd become – but she didn't. Just taking him in this one last time was a comfort.

Samuel held out his hand to her then, and she rose from the rocker. "We'll be okay," he told her. She still doesn't know if he spoke these words aloud, but she heard them all the same, heard them emanate through those lovely blue eyes, and somehow, she knew he was right.

They walked together, hand in hand, out to the crest of the wooded trail, before turning back around to stare at the beautiful old barn, reborn. "You did a nice job," she told him.

Samuel came up behind her then. He placed one of his hands on her waist, the other arm around the front of her, and he hugged her deeply into his chest. She clung to his arm and cradled it firmly atop her bosom, letting the thick, dark hair of his forearm tickle her nose. She could smell the subtle scent of lavender there.

"Sweet Viola." The words slipped from his lips like a delicate secret, and he buried his face in her hair, breathing deeply. It felt wonderful, his fullness about her, and she closed her eyes, trying to burn this feel of him into her memory. His weight against her, his breath in her hair. The smell and texture of him. Because if she did, maybe there was some way she could keep him with her forever. Somehow, the unspoken promises that hung between them would never be vocalized, because there would be no need.

"I love you, Viola." He said this last as he released her, and the warmth of his closeness left her quickly, as though a dream. He walked backward a few paces, staring at her as they drew further apart, then he stopped again, gazing past her, back toward the barn and the meadow, and it seemed as though a deep calm had washed over him just then, a sense of coming home.

Samuel started down the beach path, turning to wave one last time. Viola felt her arm raise, her palm stretch, fingers splayed to the sky, and she watched his shadow melt into the woods.

"I love you too, Samuel."

Viola cups both hands below her lips to catch her crumbling teeth.

23 July 1898

The clock in the hallway chimes 2:00 AM. Viola's eyes pop open. She is wide awake.

She lay there, momentarily thankful for the crisp cotton sheet and cozy patchwork quilt that Nonna had made for Mother and Father on their wedding day. But that gratitude quickly fades and is replaced by dread, because she has been snapped into reality and will not fall back into slumber, instead tormented by floating, surface dreams and light weeping. She does deep breathing with a degree of desperation to calm her mind so she can slip back into oblivion. It is the only time she is free from her tortuous thoughts and despair.

The moon is in waxing crescent, about a quarter full, shedding only dim light through the sash, but enough to guide her to the stairs and down to the back porch to use the privy. The door bangs shut behind her and its eerie echo is harsh on the night, which is completely silent, not even the hooting of Andie's resident barn owl. The night is dead.

She is exhausted, yet cannot bear to go back upstairs and lie in bed, willing herself to sleep for endless hours. Instead, she moves to the porch and sits in Samuel's rocker until dawn.

Despair manifests itself as tears that will no longer come, as blank, empty stares into the pasture which dissolve into one huge blob of blurry haze. Rocking ceases, then intensifies; the repetitive tap! tap! tap! of toes to board, of fingers strumming bare wood, and unconscious twirling of long, stringy hair into an oily knotted mess. Happenstance flashes of memory …

... Samuel leaning against the fence, petting Carl ...

... stretching and wiggling his toes as he sits on the porch in the sunshine ...

... lithe fingers working a potato, placing it gently in the basin ...

... a haunting glow in the dead of night, tales wept of love lost and passions wane ...

The comfort of everyday random.

Then nothing but numb.

Viola sits in Father's wing chair in the dark parlour as dusk settles upon the eve. The house is still, yet she senses a presence nearby. Lamplight spills from the open bedroom doorway directly across from her. Quiet footsteps.

Moments later, the haunting chords of a concerto drift from some distance away. Viola strains to identify the sweet melody, yet it eludes her – until -

Samuel!

She begins to rise, then abruptly hesitates, realizing the scratchy, muffled melody is not present time, rather a vinyl spinning methodically upon Mother's Victrola.

Viola settles back into the chair and catches glimpse of Samuel's naked calf and foot as he passes on the other side of the doorway.

V

30 July 1898

Viola recalls the day she walked up the stairs to deliver more blankets to Samuel; how she encountered him, shirtless, just readying to play the violin before retiring for the night. She recalls how much seeing his naked upper body stirred her; how fit and brown his chest gleamed, accentuating the shiny grey chest hairs. She realizes now there was no way he could not hear her approach, and as such could have covered himself with his shirt well before her ascent. But he wanted her to see him.

V

6 August 1898

Viola wakes from a dreamless sleep. She looks to the clock on her nightstand out of habit but remembers she has not set or wound it – any of them throughout the house – for nearly three weeks. Judging from the position of the moon, it must be around 1:00 AM. She has grown quite accustomed to telling time in this manner, as she seems to wake every hour now. It usually takes another fifteen or twenty minutes to fall back into a restless slumber each time, and this practice has bourne such weariness. She stares out the window and has a direct line to the hayloft, which once shone gentle lantern light when Samuel first arrived on the homestead. Viola closes her eyes and reaches beneath the linen. She begins to caress her breasts, remembering Samuel's soft touch, those long, elegant fingers brushing down her belly. The immediate expertise of his touch such a welcome surprise. Viola rolls over to her side and sobs.

V

13 August 1898

She lay on the bedroom floor beneath the window, a puddle of sweat and tears in the moonlight. They drip from her chin, ending in blotchy splotches which spread into the white cotton fabric of her nightgown like mini starbursts. They trail down her chin and neck, disappearing into the crack of her bosom. She hasn't washed for at least two weeks, and there is a pungent earthy smell emanating from her body. She hasn't eaten more than a few turnups pulled from the garden in the past ten days. The hunger pangs have subsided, and the weight is melting off. Her ribs are starting to show like those of a confederate prison soldier.

She walks downstairs onto the porch to survey the grounds in the moonlight.

Without proper watering, the gardens have baked away in the August sun, leaving her crops in ruin. Beans and peppers lay like wilted shoestrings on the stalk; sweetcorn pecked and gouged by the crows. The remnants of cabbage, cucumbers, eggplant and tomatoes lay in tatters, scattered across the grounds, trampled and eaten to the nibs by the chickens. Without feed, Henry and the girls dug their way out of one corner of the chicken coop and are running the grounds during the day, roosting in Andie at night. She has no idea if the brood is still intact or if the coyotes and hawks have started to pick them off, one by one. Eggs lay in the tall grass outside the barn, and inside one of the stalls, in the corner. They are piling up. Carl had broken through the wooden fence and had been on the front porch for days, baying for her, until he found his way into the hay and grain in the barn. It is scattered all across the floor, and from her bedroom window, Viola has seen rats scurrying in for a meal before disappearing back into the night. The cows are nowhere to be seen, but she imagines they must have made their way into the back pastures. The little bull is old enough now where he should be safe from the coyotes.

It is the first time Viola has stepped outside in a week. She has remained in the bedroom with the sash drawn to keep the sun at bay, sleeping and crying and willing herself to die – yet, to her dread, she always seems to wake up. Market Day has come and gone for the month. What food she had has rotted away, save for buckets of potatoes and squash in the cellar. She has been frozen, unable to go anywhere on the property because all she thinks about is Samuel. It has been just a little over a month now since his departure, and Viola's hopes for his possible return have all but faded.

And it has been over a month since Viola has walked the wooded path to the beach, the place that once offered comfort for her empty soul, now too painful to face. She hasn't been able to visit her parents, because that's where they had their picnic; when she playfully introduced him to them, and he took off his hat, bowing graciously. She hasn't entered the barn or bathed in the wash basin; hasn't been able to go up in the loft where they made love.

Viola walks off the porch and steps around the broken

chair she pitched out the bedroom window, the one where Samuel used to set his pants and hat. Oddly enough, it landed in an upright position, though one of the legs busted in half and it leans to the right. Scattered about the yard near the firepit are sheets and the dress she had worn to celebrate completion of the barn. A broken rose water decanter, and makeup crunch underfoot. She had taken Samuel's jelly jar that he left on the nightstand and pitched it out the window as well, breaking it into countless shards that twinkle in the moonlight.

Just a little over a month after Nonna Isabelle's Mourning Time, after all the visitors had departed to go on with their lives, leaving the house still and silent once more, Viola sat on Mother's lap on the front porch. Mother cradled her, gently rocking and humming. It was dark, with countless stars in the night sky.

"Madre, where is Nonna Isabelle now?"

Mother's rocking and humming stopped abruptly, and she readjusted Viola on her lap to look into her face as she spoke. She sighed heavily and cleared her throat, seeming to scan her mind for the appropriate words.

"Well, honey," she started, "our bodies are merely a vessel on this earth for something quite lovely that lives within, called a soul. Do you know what a soul is, Viola?"

Viola quickly nodded, then reconsidered and slowly shook her head back and forth, which brought a gentle chuckle from Mother.

"A soul is the true essence of a human being. It's what makes us all so special and unique, like an inner voice, right

here" - Mother touched two fingers to Viola's heart. "The soul gives us capacity for great things; to love very deeply. When a person's body dies, their soul keeps on living. It passes from the body and begins another great journey."

"Like a ghost, Mamma?"

Mother smiled.

"Sort of like a ghost, but not really. More like an incredible energy."

"What happens to the soul once it leaves the body?"

Mother looked skyward.

"Well, you see those stars up there?"

Viola gazed at the night sky, punctuated with what could be no less than a billion stars! As though God had blanketed the entire universe in midnight satin riddled with tiny pinpricks, and lantern-light from the other side shone through each minute hole to shower wonder on his complicated little creatures below.

"Every soul makes its journey to the heavens to manifest itself as one of those shining stars, full of sweet warmth and brilliance, looking down upon us, keeping us safe, and offering guidance in times of need. Whenever you feel you need to connect with Nonna Isabelle, honey, all you have to do is look to the sky, and she'll be there to shed her love and wisdom upon you like one of her big hugs."

Viola was silent for several moments as she soaked in Mother's words and contemplated the stars.

"You'll meet many souls during your lifetime, Viola. Some of them are meant to be with you just a short while, others much longer, still others forever. The most important thing is to cherish each one – to learn something from them - for it will make you a better person. The lessons are not always obvious right away; you just have to trust they will

show themselves when the time is right."

"Mamma, which one is Nonna Isabelle?"

Mother smiled warmly.

"I don't know, honey. Which one do you think she is?"

Viola pointed to the brightest star shining in the north.

"That one right there!"

Mother looked up and nodded. The smile remained on her face as a lone tear slid slowly down her right cheek. It was not until a few years later in her studies of seasons and constellations with Father that she learned the bright star she had pointed to that night was Venus, Goddess of Love and Beauty.

"Yes darling," Mother said. "I agree."

V

20 August 1898

It has been a month-and-a-half now since Samuel's departure, and Viola has accepted he is gone for good. That primitive part of her - that naivety bred deep in her veins – no longer speaks in soft whispers in the middle of the night when she lay alone in bed with the moon shining through flutters of window lace on the promise of a breeze. That has been the time most difficult for Viola, when that tiny voice inside departs rationale, feeding bits of hope and conjecture to a wounded heart. It is that time of night when she lay in bed and gaze out the window, and for just a second or two imagines the sweet melody of violin; the warm, butternut glow of lantern light announcing Samuel's return. But no more.

Viola opens the sash wide and breathes deeply. There is no sweetness on the air, as it is the time of year when everything is burnt to a crisp from the oppressive August sun. The limbs of the linden tree cast eerie tentacles on the grounds as dawn takes a foothold and Henry and the girls start to stir in the barn. It's not even 5:00 AM yet and her nightgown is already damp from the humid air which will become stifling by 10:00 AM.

A loud BANG! rattles the front door. Viola pauses to listen. Another. She walks back to the window but cannot see over the porch roof to detect what is delivering the blows.

BANG!

Viola walks downstairs and onto the porch to find Carl standing there. He sees her and lurches forward with the most pitiful bray she has ever heard.

"Oh Carl, my dearest, sweet Carl." She begins to cry as the burro buries his head in her chest. There is a healing gash on his muzzle, probably from when he broke through the fence.

"Oh sweetie, I'm sorry, I'm so, so very sorry."

Viola wraps her arms around the burro's neck and stands there, sobbing.

V

21 August 1898

The next morning she rises early and takes a bar of lavender soap down to the lake to wash the stench from her body. She ensures there is no one else on the beach and dives in, naked, letting the cool water seep into her pores and oily hair. She scrubs herself and watches the lather drift away slowly, not only cleansing her body, but removing the thick film of wanton wasteland from her mind, as well. The whispering voices and irrational fears. The longing.

Once back at the house she moves her bed to the opposite side of the room, dressing it with new linens and a different comforter. She opens the few remaining bottles of Old Overholt and dumps them off the side of the porch, then takes the empty bottles and jelly jars out back behind the barn and buries them.

Viola spends the rest of the day tidying up the house and cleaning the yard. She starts a fire in the early evening to burn the sheets from her bed, the dress and the chair. She tosses her makeup and the broken rose water decanter into the flames, which pops! in the heat.

As the fire's embers settle into a slow burn, Viola rises and stretches, and looks toward Andie. She has not been able to go inside since that horrible night in the blockhouse, when visions of blood and blinding fury haunted her dreams.

Viola takes a deep breath and slowly walks toward the entrance. She stops on the way to pet Carl, who waits for her cautiously at the corner fence post.

"My poor Carl," she says to the burro, as she scratches between his ears. He leans into the fence and blows a heavy sigh through his nostrils, then pulls away to nibble at a fresh cube of alfalfa she had wheeled into the paddock earlier that day. Although the cows seemed rather oblivious, Carl has still not totally forgiven her neglect. It would take some time for her to win back his trust – and it would certainly take a great deal of time for her to completely forgive herself.

Enough stalling.

Viola walks to the barn and lets the mammoth doors swing open wide.

Thin shafts of sunlight burst through cracks in the eaves, and the scent of fresh hay lay heavy in the barn's rafters. She stares blankly for several minutes at all of Father's lovely tools hanging on the far wall of weathered pine – the hammers, rakes, several handsaws, an ax, auger, three anvils, a posthole digger. Empty grain buckets, a wheelbarrow. Father's barn coat hangs on a horseshoe hook near the back door. She sighs.

Viola strolls the aisle bordering the stalls and takes mental note of the tasks which need attention. Clear the old bedding and lay down fresh. Sweep and shovel out the chicken poop the little darlings deposited everywhere during their freedom roam. Take a broom to the cobwebs gathering at the windowsills and the beginnings of a nasty little wasp nest in Father's old horse tack. And tiny mouse droppings scattered all about the work bench, as old Gatto had apparently abandoned the stead during Viola's leave of absence.

Viola walks toward the upper staircase and falls just short of tripping over Father's milking stool, resting squarely in the middle of the room.

"That's odd," she says, placing it under the workbench. "I don't remember leaving that there." She pauses just a moment more to curiously examine a scar on her left wrist and rubs the raised slash which has begun to ache.

She sighs, ascending the stairs.

The temperature rises as she nears the top landing, stale and stifling in the searing August sun. An elongated shadow of the far windowpane stretches across the splintered pine to stairs' edge, and she is almost hesitant to step on it.

Step on a crack – break your mother's back!

Viola moves onto the landing and surveys the sloping expanse of the loft.

The hay and alfalfa, no longer stacked ceiling high, yet still quite plentiful, occupy most of the space. Viola looks up to the ceiling and eyes the pebbled remnants of spring swallows' nests, and smiles at the memory of their graceful maneuvers. A few wasps buzz lazily near the window, seemingly drunk with the heat, and desperate for escape.

Below the window are two of Father's whiskey barrels, their brass spigots long dry and turned bronze. Atop one of the barrels is Father's old barn lantern, its handle cocked in mid-air as though waiting for her hand. Viola's footsteps strike heavy upon the smooth pine flooring, and she stops before the lantern, studying it curiously.

The lantern is thick with years of dust, though she is surprised to find a nubbin of black wick still present. She runs a finger through the dust and blows at it half-heartedly, expecting a wash of motes to tickle her nose – but the layer is so thick and caked with age, it barely produces a hint of mist.

Viola moves to the window and tries to lift the pane to let fresh air spill into the loft, but it too, is a victim of time, and her most fervent efforts produce nary a budge.

"Oh well," she muses aloud, and heads back down the staircase.

Viola walks back into the yard and surveys the outer shell of her beloved Andie. No denying she is in serious need of repair, as many of the boards suffer from dry rot, and the tin roof has long since rusted through in several places. Efforts must be concentrated here very soon. She most certainly cannot withstand many future seasons of rain and thick snow, as all the hay and alfalfa crop stored in the loft will mold and fester.

"Nothing a few new boards and a fresh coat of paint can't fix, at least for a while."

Nine

Awakening

22 August 1898, Mid-Morning

The pasture grasses are shin-high and damp. They darken Viola's Wellingtons and dungarees as she passes through them. The cows look up from their grazing and amble toward her. They follow her curiously halfway through the meadow, and old Mucca catches up, nudging Viola's pocket with flared nostrils.

"Sorry, Mucca, no goodies this morning." The heifer bellows her disappointment and slowly trails off to graze again. The others follow.

Viola reaches the end of the meadow and carefully holds down a length of barbed wire fence as she moves over it. The land is more wild and full of underbrush and berry vines here. They are quite thick in this mid-summer heat, but not too thick, as of yet, for her to pass. She readily finds the old path that will take her up through the overgrowth to the back pasture, and the clearing beyond. She's surprised the path is still here after all these years, until she remembers it is a trail

the deer depend upon to reach the sweet grass of the
meadow.

The grasses of the back pasture are even longer than those
in front. Viola has tried to alternate the cows between the
two over the years so as not to overgraze the land. "Have to
let the girls back here soon," she muses aloud.

Viola finally reaches the clearing and is somewhat
surprised to find that Mother Nature has slowly crept her
way into the open spaces here, planting maple and oak seeds
wherever she fancies, crawling from the woods on
blackberry tentacles to consume her old lilac bushes. But
time has not proven long enough for The Good Mother's
complete reclamation of what was once here.

The chimney remains a proud and stoic witness to Viola's
humble past. The red bricks are a faded pink and grey,
rounded more so at the edges, but for the most part just as
she remembers them.

*The first thing to hit her, from a distance, is the smell ...
the stench of burning wood and ash, of items both organic
and manmade. Light little tufts of ash float upon the air and
cover everything within 500 feet of her home – or what used
to be her home. What lay in charred ruins before her could
only best be described as a vague outline, or concept of what
her home had been. Looking at it now, it is quite impossible
to fathom it ever existed at all.*

*Viola stands frozen on the front stone walkway that
Robert had put in for her just last summer.*

"A tribute to my beautiful bride's endeavors."

The stones are red and grey clay, alternated in an

elaborate mosaic about her dozen or so rose bushes, or what is left of them.

Such an artist, my Robert.

She takes one step forward but cannot bring herself to take a second. It strikes her how surreal everything feels, how strangely calm and composed she is as she stands there looking at the ruins of her home. This entire moment seems to last a good twenty minutes, but in reality, must be just thirty or forty seconds in duration. Totally amazing how much information can scan through one's brain in such a brief rustling of time.

This must be the same sensation a dying man feels as his life flashes before him.

Robert and Bobby are distant and abstract to her, an attempt, perhaps, on sanity's behalf, to place them as far as possible from this still-smoldering mass of destruction.

Viola realizes she has taken several steps forward and is now just a length or two away from where the porch used to be. She and Robert sat here just last evening, sipping lemonade and watching the sun set while Bobby slept securely in his bassinet upstairs.

"Finally, some time alone with my bride."

They'd made love in the hammock that used to hang right over there, from the eves.

Viola looks down to where the hammock would have fallen, searching for some sign of its existence. A tattered length of charred rope ... a wooden grommet.

Nothing.

She is aware of the sun becoming increasingly warm, beating down atop her shoulders and head. The sky is awash in a translucent, murky haze, giving off the illusion of a burning halo about the sun. The air is very muggy and stagnant, and the closer she draws to the ruins, the harder it is to breathe. Her lungs fill with that rotten stench of burning wood, and something else - something heavy and earthy, like burnt fingernails. It is a smell she has never experienced before, but one that will haunt her forever.

The sun's position suggests it is about 10:00 AM or so. Another day in the nineties, for sure. But this close to the glowing embers, it feels like 190.

The only structure still standing is the chimney, its red brick stained with charcoal soot. A wisp of smoke wafts lazily from the top, and Viola fights an overwhelming compulsion to giggle.

Where are Robert and Bobby? In town, perhaps? Had Robert left a fire unattended in the hearth again, despite her constant protests? Did they run for help?

Viola looks up to where their bedroom would have been, where Bobby's bassinet would have rested on the table right next to their bed. She walks around the chimney toward the back side of the house, to the vicinity of the kitchen, and there, in the far corner, is part of what looks like a trundle post from their bed.

Viola is aware, on some level, that she is on the move again, but feels as though she is a spectator to herself. She continues to move deliberately around the back of the house, careful to step over charred scraps of (furniture?) and smoldering hunks of (wall?) and is keenly aware of the silence all about her, the complete and utter stillness. Not one bird chirping anywhere. No breeze, no movement whatsoever.

The world about me has died. My God, I'm the only one left.

And it is here that she finds them.

V

Late Afternoon

A gentle breeze rustles through the shells, and the crickets begin their sporadic evening symphony. Viola's favorite time of day is fast approaching, and there is one very important task which must be tended to before nightfall. It is something she has been putting off for twelve years - something that cannot go unsettled for the passing of another dawn.

Viola rises from the rocker and stretches, stiff from over a month's worth of inactivity. Placing a hand on her hip to steady herself, she walks back into the house, the familiar creaks in the flooring somehow comforting. "We're both getting on in years, aren't we, old girl?" she says, bringing forth a shy smile.

Viola takes the staircase to the upper floor and walks down to the end of the narrow hallway. There is a rope hanging from a trap door to the attic, the room that had been hers as a teenager. The walls hold the true story of her youth, promises of the future every thirteen-year-old girl waits for.

Viola in Waiting, at thirteen.

V

Viola climbs the stairs and is immediately thirteen again.

The room is totally void of furniture and fixings. She had taken all of it to her new home with Robert after they wed. But as she looks about her now, she remembers where everything once had its place, everything so neat and ordinary. The bed against the far wall, close to the window. Her nightstand right next to it, and that hurricane lamp with the spider web cracks in the flute that would cast eerie shimmers on the wall in the night. Her white dressing table over there in the far corner, covered with modest toiletries, and the armoire, filled with clothing, on the wall next to the door. And though the room is empty, it is far from ordinary.

Every inch of plaster is covered by flowers that she and Mother had painstakingly painted during the winter of 1874, right before her fourteenth birthday. *This way, we can get a head start on spring*, Mother had told her, and day after day of that long winter season, as the snowdrifts crept up to the top of the first story casements in some places, Viola and Mother created their own private world.

Tall, delicate foxglove spires wave amidst beds of cheerful woodruff and Kenilworth Ivy. Sweet William pokes its rosy face through a jungle of blackberry brambles. Pansies in every imaginable colour sprout through plumes of sand-colored sea grass, wild dandelion, and Queen Anne's Lace. Their world a combination and a contradiction; beach with desert with forest, of dreams to faraway lands and the comfort of the familiar. Of orchids and daisies and sand dunes, of golden sunlight and ocean shimmers and butterflies.

The sun has begun its slow dance into dusk, weaving its ochre glory through the branches of the linden tree next to the window. The shimmering shadows make it appear as though all the flowers are dancing in a light breeze.

Viola remembers the feel of this room as a child. The magic way the light fluttered about, warming her bedspread. The wonderful breeze wafting through the open window in spring, filling her room with the sweet scent of linden. The room is hot and stuffy now from being closed up for many years, and a thick film of dust covers the sills.

Viola walks to the closet and presses her foot into the floorboards. Somewhere ... somewhere right in this area here. This is where she used to hide her diary as a child, and Robert's first love letters to her.

Just as she considers that maybe it's sealed shut for good, her foot waivers. She bends down to pry up the loose board, and several others around it. And as she pries forth the final one, she sees it resting there, just where she had placed it twelve years ago. Robert's ammunition box.

Viola pulls the 12" x 16" pine box up from the hole and places it onto the floor, carefully replacing the loose boards. A thick layer of dust covers the box. She carefully blows it off to reveal three initials that had been burned there a long time ago: RJW.

Viola takes the box to the stairs, turning to look at her room one last time before shutting the door.

Viola stares at Robert's ammunition box, sitting atop the kitchen butcher block.

How long had she been standing there, leaning against the basin, staring at it? Ten minutes? Twenty maybe? Her whole sense of time was becoming warped.

Come visit us, Viola.

Viola speaks directly to the box.

"I know it's time," she says, slowly making her way to the porch.

Ten

Resolution

Viola carries Robert's cedar ammunition box to the porch and places it on the weathered grey pine. She sits down next to it cross-legged and drags it across the boards to rest squarely in front of her knees. The cedar is dry and splintered in places from baking in the heat of her upstairs bedroom for twelve years.

Viola closes her eyes …

… watching Robert ceremoniously pull the box from the secret cubby space below the entry staircase, just as fall harvest is nearing completion. The colors have burst upon the oaks and maples in a symphony of heartbreaking brilliance, and a coolness, full of sweet wood smoke, creeps into the early evening air through open screen doors and windows, mingling with the scent of apple pie cooling in the kitchen safe.

Robert has performed this ritual year after year, and she never tires of watching it. He places the box on the floor before the hearth and surveys its contents with the excitement of a young boy opening the first present under the Christmas tree. Carefully extracting each item. Turning it over between weathered palms and fingers. Buffing and rubbing with grease to smooth away rust and grime. Placing each one back again. Everything in order, everything in its place. This tradition of preparing for the first deer of the season is a time he looks forward to each year, a time of reflection.

"It's the connection with nature that is so inspiring my dearest, not the actual taking of the animal."

Viola's eyes snap open.

Shaking fingers lightly brush across initials burned deep into the wood. She digs into the 'R' with the nail of her index finger. "Robert," she whispers aloud, tears streaming down her blotched cheeks.

Viola flips the metal clasp and slowly lifts the lid. The scent of gunpowder is permanently baked into the wood, even after all these years. With trembling hands, she reaches for a bundle of faded yellow linen. She pushes the ammunition box aside and places the object on the porch in front of her.

"Oh," she says aloud, breath now coming in jagged sobs. Viola slowly unravels the bundle, casting the linen aside.

A scruffy little teddy bear, its tan fur coarse and well-loved. Glass brown baubles serving as eyes are dim and murky, and the corner of its left ear is singed black, almost completely gone.

Viola lifts the bear to her face and squeezes her eyes tightly shut. She buries her nose into the matted fur, breathing deeply, trying desperately to capture the sweet scent of baby that once lived there. Soft baby skin, small baby fingers, the smell of fresh powder and innocence, of fine baby hair and warm cotton blankets. But these sensations of her son have long since faded, leaving nothing but the sharp redolence of musk and gunpowder.

Her coarse wails are beyond control, and she feels as though she may go into hyperventilation, but doesn't give a damn. Her sorrow echoes into the silent yard and distant fields, amplifying her agony, all-encompassing and unyielding in its intensity. She clutches the bear to her chest, kneading and squeezing it, digging her nails into the matted brown fur.

"Bobby!" she moans, rocking back and forth and wailing.

Viola places a shaking hand back into the box and removes a violet handkerchief, which is wrapped into a small square and tied with a blue satin ribbon. She places the bear on the porch and fumbles for the corners of the ribbon, then slowly pulls on them to release the object inside. A plain gold band drops from the handkerchief and bounces onto the porch with a !ting!

She slips the ring over the identical band on her own finger and twirls it around and around, over and over, weeping. The salty tears stream down her cheeks and into her mouth. They dampen the collar of her blouse and drop into her lap, and she is unable to control them, doesn't know if they'll ever stop. She finally takes both rings from her finger and loops them through the blue ribbon, which she ties around the bear's neck. A thin pale line of white skin is all that remains on her finger.

Viola rises from the porch and walks slowly past the barn to the beach trail.

V

Dusk

Viola pulls Father's old rowboat from beneath the overgrown lake grass near the edge of the bluff. She's a bit surprised it remains intact, not having succumbed to the degradation of dry rot. Father had sent away special for this wood, teakwood he'd called it, from someplace far away and exotic.

The boat bobs at the water's edge as Viola steadies it to climb in, still clutching Bobby's teddy bear in her left hand. There is only one oar, and she uses it to push herself away from shore and slowly paddle out into the lake.

It has been a long time since she'd floated on the water. She sat beside it almost every day - in it, even, on those sultry hot evenings in the summer to cool off. But the last time she'd actually been on the water was the last time she and Father had been fishing together in late autumn before Mother's death. He had brought her out here with poles and earthworms dug by lantern light before dawn, and they floated for hours talking about Mother, about how they should prepare for the inevitable, what they would do when she was gone. She remembers being constantly aware of Mother sleeping in her chair in the parlour with a blanket wrapped around her, and how strange it felt referring to her in the past tense already, as though their vocalizing it would be Mother's curse, her demise.

Viola tucks the bear into her lap and uses the one oar to paddle herself further out, dipping it into the warm water on one side of the boat, then the other, and back again. There is no breeze, and the water is calm and sheer as ice, the screech of seagulls bouncing off its murky black surface for miles. She paddles until her arms ache, until the trees onshore are distant matchsticks. And then she lets the oar slip away beneath the darkness.

The sun has already dipped below the horizon and the sky changes colors before Viola's eyes, from a brilliant fuchsia, to deep purple. The first stars of night are shimmering.

She closes her eyes and takes a deep breath, and for the first time in as long as she can remember, all she can smell is the subtle scent of fish rising from the lake, the warm clarity of a summer evening. *Nothing more, this time. Nothing more, nothing less.*

Viola looks down at Bobby's teddy bear still cradled in her lap, the wedding rings bound by the blue ribbon to its neck. She rubs her thumb over both smooth glass eyes, and they stare back at her, blank and unknowing. She lowers the bear to the water, slowly letting its legs dip below the surface. The cotton stuffing is absorbent and weighty, and it feels as though something is pulling it down from below.

"Goodbye, my love," she whispers, letting go.

And Viola waits no longer.

ABOUT THE AUTHOR

Sandra Rubini-Rochon has enjoyed success for over thirty years as a writer, editor, artist and photographer. Her intuitive, ethereal style transcends mediums and genres, and has captured a following throughout the Seattle area and the south end of Whidbey Island - a charming, artsy enclave on the Salish Sea she has called home for three decades.